CHOICES,
REGRETS,
CHANGES

Jana Nolan

CHOICES, REGRETS, CHANGES

Jana Nolan

Earth Star Publications
Eckert, Colorado

FIRST EDITION
First Printing September 2019

ISBN 978-0-944851-58-6

Printed in the United States of America

DEDICATION

This book is dedicated to my six grown sons:

Terry Frasier
Tracy Frasier
Don Frasier
Jonathan Nolan
Jesse Nolan
Darren Nolan

The day each one of you were born my life changed. Every day has been a blessing from God, who made me your mother. My love to all of you forever.

CONTENTS

INTRODUCTION

For those of you that aren't familiar with my style of writing, or any of my books, I would like to say that this book was a different style than any other book that I have ever written. While writing, I had to become the character that I wrote about.

I grew up in a small town called Montrose, Colorado. Most of my books revolve around a small town atmosphere, but with this book I take you in a different direction.

With all of my books, I like to give you, the reader, a look at the unknown, and leave you wondering if any of it could actually happen in our time period of life.

I want you to sit back and enjoy the story that you are about to read that will give you a ride of your lifetime. When you have finished reading this book, keep in mind that this book is only fiction, or is it?

My intent as I wrote this book was focused around different choices that some of us have made in our lifetime. Most people have regrets for bad decisions, whereas others don't. Keep in mind that sometimes we are allowed to redo our bad choices and make a change, but many times we aren't able to, which can affect our life forever.

As with all of my books, I try to give my readers a lesson of what can maybe happen to them, or an idea of what someone else in their life has experienced.

The main character in this book finds himself becoming something that he isn't. Through help from an unknown object or person, he is given the opportunity to hopefully change the direction in life that he chose for himself. With this comes many emotions within this book.

Now that I have shared with you a brief summary of what the story is all about, it is up to you, the reader, to decide if any of the tales that you are about to read are capable of happening at any given moment or if they are just something that an author, such as myself, made up to captivate her readers. Fact or fiction?

Whichever way that you interpret this book, remember that there are strange happenings every day that surround us or, out of bad choices, we find ourselves in the middle of. With all of this in mind, please enjoy this fictional book that will make you think.

Jana Nolan

—1—

A BAD DIRECTION

Someone once told me that life is like a tree. Everyone begins as a simple seed, where 'roots' are our foundation or family. As a small child or sapling, a person grows straight up as our family makes their choices for us.

Once we reach early adulthood, we begin to branch out, making choices that will define the rest of our lives. Each choice that we make defines the kind of person that we want to be and shapes our soul into the kind of person that we become. It also creates or cuts off other choices that might have changed our destiny.

At times I thought that these words to me were nothing but crap, but now that I am older, I have asked myself what kind of a tree others would say that I have become with the life choices that I made for myself. I have wondered many times if I had taken my life in a different direction, what would it be like today?

Others believe that from the time we take our first breath, our life becomes our own, and what we do with it comes from the free will that God gave to each and every one of us. Some people have been able to stop in their tracks and go back to undo the damage that they have created, but for most people there is no turning back time nor changing the reality of our future as we chose it to be.

My given name at birth is Robert Frederick Stone. Throughout the years I have been called Robert, Rob, Fred, Robbie, and also names that I would just as soon forget. In other words, I have made some really bad choices, and even wishing upon a star didn't let me change any of it.

Today I went to stand at my ex-wife's grave site, where she was buried a couple of years ago. I didn't even know that she had passed away until last week, when I happened to return to the town that I grew up in. Jenny and I also lived there during the short time of our marriage.

A man who was our next-door neighbor recognized me after many years of not seeing nor hearing from me. Of course, he didn't know that Jenny and I were divorced, so he kept rattling on about how good neighbors we were and how he loved the small block dinner parties that we all had gone to, the block volleyball games that we had all enjoyed, and also that he was sorry about Jenny and my loss.

When he said this, at first I wasn't sure what he was talking about. It could have been anything. Over the years since the divorce, I seemed to have lost a lot more than I ever gained. Sometimes life has a way of doing this to a person, whether they are down on their luck or have more money than they know what to do with.

I stood there and listened to him for about 10 minutes out of respect. Here is the funny part, where I wanted to laugh, as having respect for anyone and their feelings was something that I either lost when I was young or never had as I grew older. At that moment, I interrupted the man and what he was babbling about and said, "What is it about Jenny that you are talking about? We got divorced many years ago and I haven't spoken to her since."

"I thought that you were still married. I am sorry if I offended you in anyway. Jenny died a couple of years ago. She wanted to be buried in her home town of Apple Grove, where she was born. Those were her wishes, I guess. Myself and many others assumed that you two were still together," the man replied.

I could have stood there and thanked him for his time and information about Jenny, but as I said at the beginning, I am not that kind of a person. Small talk was never my game and that was a huge problem that Jenny and I had when we were married. She always wanted to fill me in on how her day had gone or some other bits and pieces of a conversation that I cared nothing about. In fact, I felt railroaded when Jenny told me that she was expecting a child.

I never wanted children. During her pregnancy, I stayed away from her as much as I could, and when she was in labor, I made up a fake trip where I needed to go out of town on a business trip for my company, just so that I wouldn't be there at the hospital with her. Of course, I knew that at that time I was hated by her family and probably my own family wasn't very happy with me either.

In other words, I was considered a selfish, arrogant, judgmental jerk by many people, and if the truth be known, I still am. Could I ever change the history that I had written for myself? Probably not! As I get older, I realize that peace of mind is very important to me and that there might come a day when I should have tried to change and make better decisions and choices.

This is why today I am standing at Jenny's grave site, wondering what happened to her. I can hear a car with a radio blaring, coming down the dirt road that leads up here, with the person behind the steering wheel driving way too fast and this is annoying to me. When the car comes to a complete stop, I wonder why the man sitting inside the car has driven like a mad man, swerving all over the road in a cemetery. Now that he is walking up here to where I am standing, I guess I will find out why he chose to do this.

The young man is wearing a frown on his face and a chip on his shoulder. He is upset with someone or something. It is going to be interesting to find out why he is so angry.

"Are you Robert Stone?" the young man asked.

"Yes, that is one of the names that I have been referred to. I can see that you are angry and maybe you would like to tell me why. On my way up here, I don't think that I ran down anyone or caused anyone to drive off of the road, so I am confused at why your attitude toward me is this way. How do you know my name?" I asked him.

"When my mother and I left a place that we had been living at for many years, I handed out my phone number to all my friends, in case they ever wanted to call me. I was told by one of them that you had paid a visit to Kingston, where I grew up, and where you had lived for a while until you bailed out on me and my mother many years ago. I think you know who I am. I am David, Mr. Stone. The son that you deserted!" the young man replied.

"You might be right," I replied in a cold and heartless manner.

"My friend that told me that you would probably come here is the son of the man that you spoke with in Kingston. The man told his son what kind of car you were driving and a brief description of how you looked. When I saw you driving this morning, I had just come out of a store. Even with what you did to me and my mother after all of these years, I still wanted to meet the man that left us years ago! I shouldn't care, but I have never in my life met a man who is as cold-hearted as you, and I wanted to see for myself what a class act jerk looked like!" David commented.

"Now wait a minute, son!" I said.

"*Don't* you EVER call me son!" David said with anger in his eyes and voice.

"I have my reasons for leaving you and your mother. I was stuck in a marriage with a woman that bored me. She got pregnant with you and I had told her that I didn't want any kids, but she lied to me about taking precautions to not get pregnant, and then expected me to accept it and live out a life with a woman that I had no real interest in.

"I took it for as long as I could and then left to go live where nobody could ever find me that might want to collect child support for a child that I didn't want nor really care for! If you were in my shoes, you would have done the same thing!!! I came here today to see your mother's grave site, but that is the end of it. I have no regrets for what I did, in spite of many people telling me that I should have. From your temper I can see that you turned out just like me!!!" I reply.

"*Don't* you ever associate me with you! My mother raised me right with caring about other people, having respect for them and how they felt each day! I would have *never* just picked up and let my wife be alone raising a child of mine! Other people are right as you are an arrogant jerk who is going to live out the rest of your life being miserable inside and lonely as everyone around you will bore you and the truth of all of it is probably that you bore them, but they continue to put up with you out of being nice people.

"I watched Mother struggle for years as she needed help and was so disappointed and hurt by what you had done to her. She couldn't trust another man and never remarried again! I can see by your fancy car that you have done well for yourself and are a bitter, self-centered person that only puts value on objects and not what you should put it on. That, Mr. Stone, is someone helping everyone with forgiveness and understanding, and something that you will NEVER know anything about! I have said what I came here to say to you. I wish nothing but the worst for you the rest of the days that you live!" David replied with his finger pointed at my face before he walked away toward his car to leave, in hopes of never seeing me again!

The dust from the road flew through the air as David squealed his tires and drove away. This was something that let me know that he was so mad that I would not see him again. I turned around to look at Jenny's grave one last time before walking away. This time I saw a bright gold coin laying in the middle of the grass on her grave that made me question whether David had thrown it there when I wasn't looking at him, or if it just appeared magically as it was not sitting there before, when I arrived to stand there to look at her final burial place.

I didn't blame David for feeling hurt. During the time when I was growing up, I was told that I was just like my grandfather. Because he had passed away before I got to know him, I had no way of comparing him to myself. All I knew was that I did things my way for many years.

After seeing the coin, I walked over to the grass on Jenny's grave and bent down to pick it up. My intentions at the time were to give it to David, if I did happen to see him again before I left town. After I had the gold coin in my hand, my mind started playing tricks on me. I heard words that sounded like Jenny's voice talking to me. This was impossible and unbelievable!!! I was the only one standing there and the only one in the cemetery at that time who was alive!!

The words I heard were, "Robert, it's all about choices and changes. Start again."

Now I was really creeped out. A part of me wanted to take the gold coin and throw it as far away from me as I could get it, but my mind told me to hang onto it. I looked one last time at Jenny's headstone and grave.

I walked away. It was time to leave and go in a different direction than where I had just been. David was right about my fancy car and my money that I had stored in banks. I had done many things that I shouldn't have in order to have the kind of money that I had, but my life was my own and going backward in life was something that I was sure wasn't possible. Then again, I wasn't sure that was what I really wanted to do.

It was time for me to leave the cemetery. In spite of what David had said to me, I still believe that I did what I needed to do. My choices were my own.

That night I decided to stay in a motel and leave for my next destination the next morning. For a while now, I had been driving from town to town, trying to figure out if I wanted to settle down in one place for a while.

For years I have explored many different towns and cities. Some of which I was fortunate and increased my bank account. I am referring to Newark and Vegas. There was a part of me that wondered what it would be like to go back in time to my younger years, when my thoughts were formed about so many things, and try to figure out why I ended up the way that I did.

After I returned to the motel that I was staying in for the time being, I laid my head down on the end of the couch to rest for a while. I could see the bright gold coin shining brighter and flashing like it hadn't done earlier. I was tired and needed rest.

Before I went to sleep, I kept seeing myself standing over Jenny's grave and her words that she spoke to me from her grave were once again haunting me as if for some reason for the rest of my life she was going to be controlling my every move. I again heard her say, "It's all about choices and changes. Start again, Robert!"

I continued to watch the coin as it stopped flashing and was dimmer. Eventually I went to sleep.

Around 2:00 a.m. I woke up with a stiff neck from falling asleep on the couch. Over the years of making a bunch of money, I only treated myself to the best things that money can buy. I had chosen to stay in an expensive motel. When I laid down on the couch, I had no intentions of falling asleep there, but from the weird day that I had experienced, it didn't take me long to doze off.

The coin was still in my left hand. My thoughts were too wild to even think about. What I thought I had even heard in the cemetery from what sounded to me like Jenny's voice, with the coin getting brighter and brighter as it flashed, was something out of a Stephen King novel, where the coin would take over the person's mind. I wasn't going to let it do this to me! For now, I would blame this on a street light shining through my window.

Maybe there was a part of me that knew, for the first time in my life, I was experiencing a sense of guilt for what I had done to Jenny and David, and somehow because of David's words to me for the first time in my life, I did have a regret for the way that I chose to just pick up my things and get out of their lives.

Then my next thought was NO! There is no way that I was that kind of a guy! I had done many things in my lifetime that I should be ashamed of. My heart feels nothing for what I have done wrong.

I got up from the couch and went to the dresser, where I had thrown the coin. I would leave it there until I got ready to check out of this place, which would maybe be in a few days. I had decided to stay for a short time longer. After what happened yesterday, I knew that I wouldn't be going back to the cemetery.

I grabbed my leather jacket and car keys. I left my room to go to an all-night truck stop that I was sure would be open and ready for business. I needed coffee and something to eat.

As I was driving down the street, I saw a young man that reminded me of how I was at his age, when I was hanging out with my friends in the early morning hours, when I should have been home instead of out on the streets. The young man was leaning up against his car, smoking a cigarette, and drinking what appeared to be a bottle of beer. His radio was turned up as loud as he could get it, listening to something that I wasn't familiar with.

As I waited for the stop light to turn green, I saw some girls and other guys drive up in their cars to get out. They walked over to the young man to join in to what appeared to me to be a party waiting to happen.

Every one of them looked at me and continued talking. I would not be surprised if they were referring to me as the old man watching and annoying them as I had been looking their way. The truth is, for a brief moment I felt like I was living a part of my past.

The light turned green and I continued to drive, looking on both sides of the street. It was much easier finding the truck stop during the day than during the early morning hours when most people are sleeping or should be, anyway.

While driving, I remembered a building on the corner of

where I was to make a right turn. From there it wouldn't be long and I would be at my destination.

The place was lit up, and many trucks were parked there either with the drivers inside eating, or some of the truck drivers sound asleep in their rigs. There was an open spot in front across from the front door. I was able to watch from inside to make sure that no one tried to break into or do anything bad to my car.

After entering, I stood and waited a couple of minutes until I was seated by a window at a small table. The waitress was nice and not bad to look at. If I was going to stay here in this town for a while, I might have asked her out. I saw that there was no ring on her finger, letting me know that she was married. There was no way that I wanted to complicate my life with a woman hanging all over me and begging me to stay! I was a loner. I had been for many years. More than likely, I would continue to be this way the rest of my life.

When the waitress returned, I ordered four eggs, hash browns, ham, toast and coffee. All of this food would hold me over until it was time for dinner.

I had the feeling that once in this lifetime I had been in this town before, or who knows, maybe a previous lifetime. Something seemed familiar to me, but yet I couldn't understand why. Maybe when I was growing up, my parents drove through here. For some reason this town, or the people that lived in it, fascinated me. It's not the friendliest town that I have been in, but there definitely was something that was keeping me here for a couple of days. I was hoping that before I got ready to leave, I had figured everything out, and the reason why I even wanted to be here for as long as I did.

After I was done eating, I went to the cash register to pay. When I reached into my pocket to grab my wallet, I pulled out the same coin that I had thrown on the dresser! I hadn't picked it back up. My thoughts now were that for some supernatural way, this coin was meant to stay with me. *Why?* Was it supposed to be a good luck charm of some sort, or a reminder of Jenny and what I had done to her, and

David? After all, I did find it laying on the grass, on top of her plot that she was buried in. I guess the reasoning behind the coin would present the truth, and it all would come out in the scariest way possible!

When I drove away, I decided that I would drive around for a while to check out the town, to see what it had to offer. For now, I had all of the time to spare in the world and wasn't in a hurry to leave.

There was a reason why the coin got brighter and flashed. If I couldn't figure this out soon, I felt like it was going to drive me crazy!!

The more I drove around and looked at different buildings and streets, the more I realized that I had at one time or another been here at least one other time. During the time that Jenny and I were married, we hadn't come here to visit any of her friends or family that at that time lived here.

When I was working, none of my construction jobs had taken me here. Was it the coin that I seemed to be attached to that wouldn't leave me, now making me think the thoughts that I am or was at one time or another, when I was either too small to remember or during a life that I didn't remember bringing me here to either live or work, as I was now seeing places that were very familiar to me.

I am sure that some people would probably think that I had lost my mind, but I was trying hard to believe that I hadn't. As far as I know, there was only one other time in my life when anyone questioned my stability and mindset, and this was when I worked for a big company called Russ-A-Thon. It was a fabric textile and upholstery company that was built many years ago in Newark, New Jersey.

After I left Jenny, the night she went to the hospital, I went as far East as I could possibly go, in hopes of no one finding me. I even gave up contact with my own family because I didn't want to be found. There was too much baggage that could be following me with child-support, attorneys and others that, at that time, would just as soon kill me rather than look at me. I have been a con artist and player for many years. At Russ-A-Thon I was a CEO.

It was strange how I got the job of CEO as I didn't work my way to the top or have experience in anything that pertained to fabric, upholstery or textiles. I hadn't gone to a business school, college or university.

The day that I got the job, I was sitting on a park bench, looking through a newspaper, trying to find work. I thought the best that I would find might be a construction or a steel worker job. Newark was a huge city. I knew that there was plenty of opportunity there waiting for me. When I saw the ad about Russ-A-Thon needing help, I thought that maybe it might be for something simple that would keep me going until one of the other jobs that I would apply for would get in touch with me.

At the time, I did have a telephone in my seedy motel room that was in a bad part of Newark, which I referred to as home at that time, where I could make and receive calls. The lady at the front desk seemed to have a thing for me.

The day that I arrived at the motel and was standing there paying for my room, the young woman taking care of the front desk kept looking at me and smiling. In fact, she even rubbed up against me a few times. She was interested. I knew that I wasn't going to be lonely if I chose not to be. Since my phone calls had to come through the front desk operator, who was responsible for transferring the calls to my room, the lady clerk agreed to take messages for me when I wasn't there. She knew that I was looking for a job.

I am tall, with coal black hair that now has some gray in it, blue eyes, broad shoulders, and like I said, a great-looking body, not to mention a gorgeous smile. With my looks, there was no doubt that I was going to get a job somewhere and I was willing to do whatever it took to get one.

So, after I had circled the job for Russ-A-Thon in the paper, I also circled a few more jobs. There were a couple of construction jobs available, and also an opening for a steel worker. I noticed some bartender jobs that I was sure I could get, but with these mostly I would be relying on my tips, and I wasn't sure that would pay the kind of money that I wanted. I was going for the big money and wasn't going to settle for anything else.

I wanted to look my best when I went to apply for every job I saw in the paper. I went back to my room to clean myself up before traveling to the different companies. Waiting in my room was the lady that took care of the motel front desk. She had come to visit me.

Let's just say that she wasn't disappointed with her visit after she had left. As I stood there at my motel room door, letting her out, I had a smile on my face, but it was more of a cocky smile as, like I said, I had no regrets and thought at that time that I was God's gift to women.

I showered and got dressed up to once again leave to apply for each job. I knew that I would come back here with something as I could sell ice to an Eskimo. I was a fast talker and knew that whatever came out of my mouth, whether it be the truth or a fabrication, would land me a well paid job and life.

My first stop was at the construction companies. I had years of experience working for a construction company, but by the time I walked out of there, I had made it seem like I had been a well paid foreman for the company. I gave out fake addresses and phone numbers listed that I was sure that they wouldn't check up on to see if I was telling the truth.

Then it was on to a big building to apply for the steel worker job. The same pile of horse crap came out of my mouth with lies, fake companies that I had worked for, and phony phone numbers to go with it of people that I knew. I was sure that I would get a call from them.

Like the lady at the front desk in the motel office, the receptionist kept looking at me and smiling. I could see that there was a good chance that she would move my résumé to the top of the list and maybe even talk the head honcho of the company into hiring me.

As you can see, everything was always about me and what I wanted in my life, whether it be good or bad, but unfortunately, David was the bad part of my life that I didn't want, and there were no regrets on me leaving and running far away from there, and everyone.

So, then my next stop was at Russ-A-Thon. I by then had fabricated so many stories about myself that seemed to come easy to me that this was going to be a piece of cake pulling the wool over their eyes.

After I got called in to talk to the owner of the company, Ted Jones, I made it sound like I had done this type of work for years and made huge profits for the companies that I had so-called worked for. I had him under my thumb and he said that he was very impressed with everything that I had done and that he was looking for an office assistant, but that he also was wanting a new CEO.

After talking to me, he was thinking that he would hire me as the CEO as he was highly impressed with my way of doing things in business. He said that he was putting his faith in me as he was sure that with all of my experience that I would take his company very far.

At one point of him bragging on me, I felt like laughing as I had told him nothing but garbage. He was sucker enough to believe everything that came flying out of my deceitful mouth! At that moment is when I realized that I was born to be a con artist, scammer and a player.

Instead of laughing, I shook his hand. I told him that he had made a very good choice and that I wasn't going to let him down. He told me that the job came with big bucks and those were the words that I wanted to hear. I would choose my hours of work and sit back to watch the dough pile up in my bank account.

I walked out of the owner's office with my smirky smile. Before I left the room, I told the receptionist that I would see her in the morning. Once again, she smiled at me, and I could see that she was going to be easy to fool as well as the owner.

Like I said, I knew that I would get a job that day. My next stop was a fancy restaurant, where I ordered the biggest steak that they had with all of the sides that went with it. I was on my way to success. I wasn't going to let anything stand in my way of having everything that I wanted, and needed.

After feasting on the steak and sides, I went back to my room to sleep. I knew that before long, I would be making so much money that I could afford an expensive penthouse or a huge condo in the best neighborhood of Newark. My dreams of being stinking rich were someday going to come true. Nothing, or no one, was going to stop me from getting what I wanted.

The next morning when I woke up, I was showering and getting ready to put on the nicest suit that I owned, which happened to be the one that I had worn to Jenny's and my wedding. Before the wedding, I had also bought a name-brand pair of shoes as I wanted to stand out in my appearance and look my best from top to bottom. I wanted to impress everyone that came to the ceremony to watch Jenny and I say our vows and promise each other that we would stay together the rest of our lives.

This turned out to be a crock as the marriage started going downhill fast. It was a little after a year when we were apart. Our divorce soon followed.

Jenny and I had met five years after I had graduated from high school in my hometown called Kingston. Both of us were 23 years old. She was working as a waitress. I was working for a small construction company, driving a skid-steer. I won't tell you that it was love at first sight as it was everything *but* that.

In fact, the night that we met, she was walking past me, carrying way too much. I was sitting at a table, looking at a menu, when Jenny slipped from water that was spilled on the floor. When she went down, the coffee that she was carrying not only spilled on me, but also on her, along with the food that she was carrying. I was somewhat upset as the coffee was hot, but when I looked down and saw her on the floor, I got up from my chair and helped her up. We both ended up laughing at each other as we were a sight wearing coffee and food.

We had many conversations thereafter for a while, which led to one thing and another. Before we knew it, I had asked her out on a date. We were both young. Jenny was new at her job and the work force. We spent a bunch of time talking about how we ended up at the jobs that we had.

Jenny was beautiful. She had blond hair with green eyes and a smile that at that time made me smile. In other words, she was gorgeous. I was getting closer to her as she was to me. After a few months of dating, I asked her to marry me.

We were living in a very small apartment with a hundred steps to walk up and down, leading to and from the place we called home. She continued to keep her job as I did mine. For a month or two, everything was going well with us. Then came the day when I arrived home from work, tired and hungry from my hot and humid day in the sun, to find that she hadn't cooked anything for us to eat.

At first when she announced that we were going out to eat, I wondered why. She explained that she had some great news to share with me, and that night out was going to be a celebration for us. My first thoughts were that maybe she had gotten a raise in pay or found a better paying job, so I agreed to go.

After we got all dressed up and were sitting at the restaurant, Jenny told me that she was pregnant. I was very upset. I stood up from my chair and shouted out the words, "You're WHAT?" Of course, this drew attention to everyone around us, and all heads and ears were focused on our conversation until we had eaten and left.

The drive back home was a quiet one. I had talked to Jenny about my feelings about us having kids before we were married, and told her that I didn't want to be a dad. At that time, she had told me that she would respect my wishes, and would take precautions so that it wouldn't happen. When I reminded her of the agreement to use precautions, she just said that sometimes things happen, and that what was used to keep her from getting pregnant must have failed to work. She then started crying as she could see that I was very mad at her.

I think at that moment is when I decided that there would come a time very soon when I would be packing my bags and going as far away from her as I could get. Of course, her family and mine were very happy to hear the news. Whenever any of them tried to talk to me about how fortunate Jenny and I were to be expecting a bundle of joy, I chose to change the subject as I knew my feelings weren't going to change.

Jenny became more excited every day as the baby grew inside her. After she was six months along, she almost lost the baby. The doctor told her to stay off of her feet as much as she could until after the baby was born. This put an extra burden on me as I had to work more hours in order to keep the bills paid and food on the table for us to eat.

With each passing day, I became more bitter and couldn't wait until I could get out of there. I managed to save some money from her for gas when I felt that it was time for me to hit the open highway going East.

Jenny's happiness about having a baby soon increased more so than before. Our love-making had stopped, and me being a man with needs, I decided to leave in the middle of the night and go to a club to find companionship for the night. Jenny was fast asleep and that was my perfect opportunity to do this at that time.

There were many women there that were happy to see me. So, I had my pick of the litter. I managed to sneak back into the apartment before she woke up. After fixing my lunch, I was on my way to work. There were many other nights after that one when I left while she slept.

This was working out good until a man that I knew saw me in the club and told his wife about where he saw me, and also what I was doing there. His wife couldn't wait to tell

Jenny. By then Jenny was almost nine months pregnant. When she heard the news, she realized that I wasn't the nice, faithful husband that she thought that I was.

We had a huge fight, and she bent over in pain. She was in labor. She told me to drive her to the hospital. I told her that I would have to call a taxi for her as I was scheduled to go out of town on business for the construction company. That I had to do this as we would need the extra money even more after the baby was born.

Once again, Jenny cried and asked me not to leave. I told her that I had no choice. When the taxi arrived, I told the driver to take her to the hospital and help her. I also asked him not to leave her until she was in the hospital and with a nurse or doctor. The taxi driver agreed to do this, telling me what a lucky man I was to be having a son or daughter soon.

I just nodded and told him not to waste any time getting her there. When they left, it was time for me to finish packing everything I wanted to take with me, and leave the apartment, which would be just the right size for Jenny and her baby.

That night I stayed in a cheap motel. In the morning, I went to an attorney to do the paperwork for the divorce. The attorney was confused as to why I would do this after just becoming a father, but my words to him were that I had for years believed that any man could father a child, but that didn't make him a father, and that I could never be one.

The attorney finished the paperwork. I signed it. I gave him a fake address where I would be living, telling him that I would be contacting him and for him not to contact me as it would be hard to reach me as I wouldn't have a phone for a while.

I let him know that I was quitting my job and would be looking for one in another town. He told me that he would serve Jenny the papers, but it wouldn't be until after she had gotten home from the hospital. Once she had signed them, it wouldn't take long and the divorce would be done and over with.

These were the words that I wanted to hear.

I then went to the construction company, quit my job, and got my last paycheck that was coming to me. I knew that Jenny's parents would help her with money until she could work or collect money from the state. My concerns were just on myself and no one else.

When I stopped to get gas, I ran into a guy that Jenny had worked with and had introduced me to. He congratulated me. He said that he happened to be at the hospital last night and had heard that Jenny and I had a baby boy. He said that I must be beaming inside from happiness. I just looked at him, climbed into my car, and drove away going East.

Within a few months, I had called the attorney, who told me that Jenny had signed the papers and that the divorce was final. I was a free man. You would think at that moment I would be ashamed of myself for what I had done and have regrets, but I continued to feel nothing inside. Like I have said, I have no regrets.

After a while on the road, with many stops along the way, I was then living in Newark. It was time for me to go to work and see how many of the people working for this company that I could fool for the day, month, year, or as long as I chose to be there.

I looked good, walked tall, and smiled big when I entered the building. My receptionist had a smile again on her face that told me that she was happy that I got the job. I was sure that she had other thoughts on her mind as well. I found out what the owner needed me to do for the day. I sat down at my nice desk. I made several phone calls to many people, building up the company with words that only a fast talker could speak. I was good at it. Before the day was done, I had many contracts and more money coming into Russ-A-Thon's bank account and mine. I was told by the owner the account number for the company bank account. I also was given permission to withdraw money at any time if I needed to do a wire transfer, and to use his name as being the one authorizing the transfer as he was a busy man and not at the company that much. This was the open door for me to put large amounts into an account that I had set up with a fake name that belonged to me.

When the owner, Mr. Jones, heard the good news and how good of a job that I had done for him and the company that day, he was overwhelmed. He gave me a big pat on my back and a firm handshake. He told me that he had no regrets hiring me, and again I wanted to laugh as I had no regrets being there at this company, getting money for not just the owner, but a huge amount for myself wherever I could get it.

—2—

DECEIT AND MORE

Once again, I walked out of my office, straight and standing tall, feeling confident that I had successfully talked many people into either buying into Russ-A-Thon or wanting to sign a contract, allowing them to sell products that this company offered. I knew nothing about the crap that I was telling many people, but the good part of it, at least where I was concerned, was that the people buying my lies didn't know this.

I looked over at the receptionist and told her that I would see her in the morning. From there I went to a different fancy restaurant to eat and sit, to think about what else I could do to increase my bank account.

Every day it was the same thing. I would go to work and make more money for the company. The owner was so pleased with me that with the nice big check that I was given each week also came with a huge bonus check for all of the great work that I had done for the company.

I had gone from just a small amount of money for gas that I had saved back from Jenny before I left her, to a huge amount of money showing in my bank account. It was time for me to move out of the dive motel and into an expensive home. I had been looking at many different penthouses, houses and condos, trying to find the perfect one that would fit my personality and also my bank account. After several days of looking, I found a penthouse in the best part of the city, where only rich people stay. It was furnished with only the finest and that was what my ego wanted. My life had really gone from rags to riches. There would be no more living in a small dumpy apartment for me.

Because of the job, I had made several new friends that were from the best and wealthiest families in Newark. I had even suckered some of them into investing in Russ-A-Thon. Every night there was a different woman who would come by to keep me entertained, or should I say *me* entertaining her. I had the kind of life that I had dreamed about for years, and it seemed like things were getting better and better for me. This was my life for a few years until I woke up one day.

I was sitting on my couch, looking through the paper, when I read something that surprised me and made me wonder what was going to happen next. The Stock Market had crashed and Russ-A-Thon could be in danger of going under. I needed to shower, dress and get to work very soon to see what the next plan was that concerned that company.

That day, when I walked through the door next to my office, my receptionist wasn't smiling. In fact, she had a cold look on her face. I didn't know what to expect on the other side of the door to my office, but would find out soon. When I opened it, I was surprised to see Mr. Jones sitting at my desk. He, too, wasn't smiling. This looked bad for me!

"Robert, I see you came to work today. I have something to say to you that you won't want to hear. I had a lot of complaints from many companies and people that you had signed up under contract to either be an investor, or companies that at the time thought that they were going to be able to put their logo on the products that we furnish. In other words, Robert, you lied to them! You have been here for several years now and I can't believe that I didn't catch this before now! My answering machine has been overloaded from calls, telling me that they were deceived and are getting an attorney to sue me in court for false representation.

I was a fool the day that you walked into my office, Robert! Instead of checking out your résumé then, I believed all of the lies that you told me, and hired you! Since early this morning, I did refer back to your résumé, and found out that these so-called companies that you listed didn't even exist —just like the fake names and phone numbers for the people that you put down as contacts. In other words, Robert, you are a con artist, and a sleaze bag that is a fast talker to get what you want in the process of taking advantage of good, honest people and me—the owner of this company! I have a bunch of money to give back now. I have contacted my attorneys, who are going to make you pay for what you have done to me!" Mr. Jones said.

"I did what I felt needed to be done at the time as your company wouldn't have existed this long without me taking charge and doing this. The Stock Market has crashed, and this company would have been out of business anyway as of today. You will lose everything regardless!" I had said with a cocky voice.

"Yes, the Stock Market did crash, but it didn't hurt my company. The only thing that did hurt me was me believing you. You have five minutes to gather all of your stuff and get out of this office. You have a serious problem, Robert, and need to seek mental help as you think it is all right to take advantage of people and try to ruin them. If I can't straighten this out on my own, I have attorneys that will come after you for every dime that I have to pay back to all the people that you misled. What you did was called fraud, Robert!" Mr. Jones replied with an angry look.

"There was no conversation recorded with these people or companies. With the stamp that was used at the bottom of the contracts, there is no way that you or your attorneys could prove that I was the one that had given them false information. The name on the contracts is your name and not mine. If you take me to court, you will be the one leaving there crying and not me. Think about it!" I said as I laughed all the way out of the office door and the other door leading out of my receptionist's room.

Now my thoughts were going in a different direction. I had a huge penthouse to sell if I needed or wanted to, and money in the bank that I needed to use sparingly until I could buffalo someone else into hiring me. This was my last thought about that time in my life for me, but I knew there would be more to come.

As I drove around, looking at the town, remembering my life with Jenny and what had transpired after I had traveled to Newark and what I had done to get the well paid job at Russ-A-Thon, I was needing to go back to the motel and try to sleep.

The flashing coin that wouldn't just disappear or leave me was causing me to remember many things about myself and my life choices that I had chosen for myself. The life I had in Newark was just a small segment of my earlier years of life. At that time, I was cocky and full of myself. That part of me hasn't changed.

With the coin that I found on Jenny's grave and the words that she spoke to me from her grave, it made me wonder if she was telling me that I had better find a way to change my way of thinking, my lifestyle and choices that only went bad and still do at times.

There is a reason why I had turned out the way that I did. Someday, maybe I would know the reason, but for now, I had to realize that I am who I am and keep going.

After going inside my motel room, I once again took the coin out of my pocket and set it on top of the dresser. It kept flashing and was brighter than it had been. I went to my window and looked out at the street to see if there was something out there that could be reflecting on the coin to make it look like it was flashing. There was nothing out there!

Whatever this was seemed more to me to be supernatural ,and it was freaking me out more so than it had before. I sat on the couch, watching it until it finally went dim again. This was a mystery that someday would be solved, but when?

This night I went to the bed to sleep. As I laid there watching the coin, I found myself thinking about what took place after I had walked out of Russ-A-Thon that day.

I was sure that Mr. Jones wouldn't take me to court. If it was true and the Stock Market crash didn't affect his company, he didn't want the bad publicity that would be all over the newspapers. It would be hard for him to prove that I was the only one involved in this.

I had no regrets for what I had done. It bought me an expensive penthouse and also had given me plenty of money in my bank account. I had taken my life in the direction that I wanted it to be the day that I walked into that company to apply for the job. The fear that he was trying to instill in me didn't work.

Once again I went to an expensive restaurant to eat dinner. Just because I was now jobless, I could still afford the luxuries of life. Sometimes going places where the rich go can be a good thing, and a place to meet important people that can offer you more than what you would have had before you went there.

After I ordered and was sitting there waiting for my food, an older man and woman that I had seen and talked to before walked over to me.

"Mr. Stone, I see that you decided to eat out as we did tonight," the man said.

"Yes, I like to try new restaurants and this is the first time that I have come to this one. I've heard nothing but good reviews about it, though," I replied.

"My wife and I eat here often, and yes, their food is as good as you have heard it to be. I remember you telling me that you work for Russ-A-Thon. When the Stock Market crashed, did it affect this company?"

"No. It is still in business," I replied.

"That's good. Years ago, I wanted to be a stock broker. It appears that this is the type of job where big money is made. My wife talked me out of doing this as she said that it would occupy most of my time, and I wouldn't have time for her," the man said, laughing.

"She might have been right. This is why I am not married," I said, laughing as well.

By then, the waitress had brought my food. The man and lady that he was with, whether it be his wife or his lady friend, told me to have a nice evening. They walked away.

What the man had said stuck in my mind. I didn't need to work for someone else. I had money enough in the bank to set myself up in a nice building and be a stock broker. With my personality and being a fast talker, I could con my way into being a successful stock broker without an education or a license. With the crash that had just happened, I could promise the people that I came in contact with the world. They would invest in whatever crap I decide to sell them.

I finished my meal and went back to my penthouse to sleep. Tomorrow was going to be the first day of Rob Brown, the stock broker, and a way to increase my income. The people that I sold the crap to wouldn't have a clue exactly where their money was going to or whose bank account it would be going into. Which would be mine. I would require cash only from them.

When morning came, I was up early and on my way to once again a real estate agency, to see if there was a small building that I could rent in a good part of Newark from month to month. I was good at giving out false information and names, so this would be a piece of cake for me. I was stopping at my bank to draw out money enough to give to the Realtor in hopes that she wouldn't need to see a driver's license.

My plans were to also make up a huge lie as to what I would be selling in there. Then I was going to hand out business cards with, once again, a fake name.

All of this sounded good in my mind, but was it going to work? After the first month, I would know. At that time, if this idea of mine wasn't going as good as I thought that it would, then I would close, and lock the door with an OUT OF BUSINESS sign on it, and once again start looking for a job.

When I entered the Realtor's office where I hadn't been before, I was smiling. So was the lady behind the desk.

"Hello, can I help you with something?" the lady asked.

"Yes, I am looking for a small building in the best part of Newark to rent from you on a month to month basis. I have placed an ad on a website. I have some things that I want to sell. What I am selling isn't anything of value, but things that I want to get rid of," I said.

"Well, that might be nice if you could turn the building into a small thrift store. There might be other people that are interested in getting rid of a bunch of things that they have no use for any longer, and they might be willing to bring their stuff to you to sell for them," the lady commented.

"You could be right." I told her as once again I was holding back laughter. There was no way that I was going to have a business like that! I was way too good for that!

"I am sure that I can find you a small building in the better part of Newark to rent. Where you are wanting to rent month to month, I don't see any reason to have you sign a contract with us. All I need is your name, address and a phone number, in case I would need to call you," she said.

"My name is Rob Brown. My address is 643 Peaceful Lane, and my phone number is a cell phone. The number is 287-8645. It will be hard to get a hold of me as I will be working. I will check in with you from time to time and keep in touch. Thank you for your help," I said with a smile on my face, knowing that I had deceived this lady and that I was planning on raking in more dough than she could make in a lifetime.

Once again, I had scammed someone into believing me. Years ago, when I met Jenny, I wasn't like this. I was honest with everyone that I knew and saw. The day that I left Jenny was the day I realized that nice guys finish last, and believing Jenny's words and trusting her to keep her word was a bad choice and mistake!

The lady Realtor looked up all the small buildings that were available. She told me that she had found the perfect one for me. I paid her for the first month of rent plus a deposit for any damages that could occur. She said that I would get back the deposit when I brought her back the keys. She then handed me the keys and told me the directions to the building that was in the best part of Newark.

My next stop was at a place that made business cards for people. I told them to make me a hundred of them with the same name that I had given the Realtor lady. The name Rob Brown sounded like it had some class to it and would be easy for everyone to remember. I paid the clerk for the cards. When he handed them to me, I could see that they were very professional. At this moment I was making progress and at the top of my game.

For the next few days, I read and studied the Wall Street page of the newspaper, to see if the Stock Market had pulled itself back up again from the crash. If it had managed to do this, I wanted to see what stock was the hottest right now. This was not the first time for the market to crash. I needed to know which stock was climbing to the top.

I read where Wall Street was in full force once again. It was time for me to go to work. I started making phone calls to rich, important people whose names and phone numbers I wrote down from the office at Russ-A-Thon.

That night I went to a different fancy restaurant, where I had never been before, in the best part of Newark. I handed out my cards to everyone that I could talk to. I shook their hand and told them that if they wanted to make more money that I was the one to see. Also, that I knew the right stock for them to buy shares into. With their investment, I bragged to them, saying that they would double or triple their earnings. I assured them that I would keep them updated on when the right time would be to sell and not lose any of their money.

Before I walked away, I shook their hand again and told them that I was their man that they needed on their side. If I didn't know better, I would think that I was standing there promoting myself in order to get their vote as if I was running for Mayor of Newark or maybe Congress.

Instead, I was just a con man that loved money!

Several people sounded interested as they knew that the Stock Market had made a turnaround and was back in full force. I had even made some appointments to have them come to my office, where I could talk to them about what stock they should buy and invest in.

I had reviewed the Wall Street page every day with the top stock that seemed to be really doing good and climbing upward. I knew that in order for me to be able to pull this off, I had to know what I was talking about or the people that I saw would catch on to me right from the beginning as they had dealt with stock brokers before.

I had done plenty of research. I also was going to tell them that I didn't trust banks as banks have a way of failing and that I wasn't about to lose any of my money or theirs. That I only would take cash from them, I said that I would give them a receipt for their money that they had given to me to invest for them, and that I would send them out a weekly report showing how their stock was doing. That I was their man that they needed to do this for them.

Once again being deceitful. So far, my money had increased with all the conning that I had done, but if I wasn't extra careful, it would take a turn, and I would get caught and locked up for a long time!

I continued to do my homework. I had listed on paper every stock that continued to stay at the top of the list. That day there was a man who had made an appointment with me that would be coming to talk to me. I had furnished the small building with expensive furniture. I even added some flower pots to help dress the room up with a nice desk, computers, copying machine and file cabinets. I had turned the small room into an actual office that looked like I had been there for quite a while, where I continued to work at my prosperous business.

I had to put on a show as no one was going to hand over cash to a man in an empty room and believe what he said to them. I was all set up and ready for business with a cheap cell phone that I could throw away at any time.

Around 2:00 p.m., a tall younger man that looked rich opened the door and saw me sitting at my desk. I stood up and shook his hand. I told him to have a seat and I would get started.

"I'm glad that you decided to come see me today. You made the right choice," I said, smiling.

"As I told you, Mr. Brown, I am a busy man. I came here today to see you so that I could hear what you have to say. Right now, I am ready to buy shares in stocks again. With everything that you have told me the last couple of times that we have talked, I am confident that you could be the broker that I have been looking for and need. Now all I need is for you to recommend what stock you feel is on its way to the top, and will be there for quite a while. I am all about making more money. If you can do this, then we are on our way and can get started," the man replied.

"Well, to be honest with you, you have made the right choice. I have been in this business for many years now. I won't let you down. If you decide to go with me, I have to let you know that I only take cash, which I will buy your investments with. I learned years ago that banks have a way of going under. I have been discouraged ever since with having a checking account. I keep my money in a safety deposit box at a bank. This might sound strange to you, but with me doing this for years, it has always been the best choice for me. I will give you some paperwork to take with you. Also, each week I will send you an update on where your stock is going. If at any time I feel like it is time for you to sell and maybe buy into a different one, then always remember that I will let you know. I, too, am a busy man and it is hard to reach me on my phone. If for some reason you need to speak with me and I don't answer, leave me a message. I will get back to you as soon as I can," I said.

"This all sounds convincing to me, Mr. Brown. I am ready to look at what you suggest and pick some stock that I am interested in and you feel would be best for me." He commented.

At that moment I showed him a paper that looked very professional that I had created with all of the products, companies, etc., that were listed on the Wall Street page. I told him which ones were doing the best at the moment and what I would recommend.

It must have been enough for him to see as he pulled out his wallet and asked me where he needed to sign on the paper that I had made up, along with many pages that had mumble jumble on them. In other words, everything that he had was a fictitious contract that had words on it that came from my imagination and wouldn't stand up in a court of law, yet looked professional.

The man had picked out a couple of shares and signed his name. He was happy with his choices and with me. This time he was the one first to shake my hand before he walked out the door. I was not only a con artist, but also a player playing with his money as my next stop would be me taking it to my bank to deposit it as he walked out of my office, feeling like I had helped him to become even richer than he already was.

The truth was that *I* was the one richer than I was before he left as *I* was holding onto his $20,000 in cash. Not bad for a day's pay.

This continued several times that week with other rich people taking a chance on me and putting their trust in me. I had scammed many people and was increasing my bank account by leaps and bounds. I also had sent each one of them updates that I had made up. I did this so that they would keep coming back again, wanting to buy into more shares of the same stock or a different one.

At the end of the month, I had raked in $500,000 and was sitting pretty good. I continued to watch the Wall Street report every day, to make sure that what they had bought into for all of their shares was on the up and up and was still doing good. I had even called each one of them from the disposable phone, telling them that their investments were doing great.

Word had traveled and I had many other rich people coming to my office to buy into the Stock Market. My life was sitting pretty. I didn't need to work for someone else other than myself. I was the one in control. With me being a fast talker, I kept raking in more money each month. If things kept going the way that they were now, I would be stinking rich!

Knowing sooner or later, though, that there was a good chance that I would get caught at my own con game, I decided that after another month of taking these innocent people for a ride, I would need to suddenly come up missing.

When this happened, it would mean dyeing my hair to a different color, growing a beard, changing my style of clothing that I wore each day, buying a cane to use and also a fake pair of glasses. My appearance was going to change a lot. If the people that I did deceive went to the authorities with a description of me, I would be hard to find. If I had to, I would even leave Newark for a while until things cooled down for me. Now was the time to play it safe and not make any mistakes.

Like every con artist, I was greedy and continued for a few more months doing what I had been doing, and taking a chance on getting caught. At this time everyone was content and happy as they could see that their stock was going through the roof and growing each day.

Something finally told me that it was time to stop and I had to go with my instincts. So, I took this a different way. I typed out many professional letters to all of the people that I had scammed and told them the name of an actual broker. I told them that I had informed him about them and that I wanted to make sure their investments were kept safe. That the other broker would let them know when or if it was time to sell or trade stock. He would be in charge of their money now. I knew that what I had told them was a lie and that I had all of their money. I had to give myself some time before the heat could start coming down on me.

I hired someone to come to the building to take out all the furniture and flower arrangements and give it all to a charity of some sort. I also disposed of anything and everything that could relate back to me. I stomped on the cheap phone and after I left, I threw it away in the nearest dumpster. I had put an OUT OF BUSINESS sign on the door and dropped the keys in a night deposit box that was attached to the Realtor's office with a typed note, stating that I would no longer be renting the small building. As for the deposit that was supposed to come back to me, I didn't care about it and thought it would be best not to show my face there again.

From there I went to a store and bought hair color and everything I would need, including some dumpy looking clothes and a cane.

After I had finished doing this and walked out of my penthouse, I had neighbors who thought that I was a different man who was living there now. I had fooled them as well. My appearance had changed. It would stay that way for days, months, or however long it took until I was certain that I was safe and no one would recognize me. I would continue to stay in Newark for a while longer.

—3—

WHAT HAPPENED TO ME

All of this and what I had done was coming back to me and stuck in my mind. I laid in bed for as long as I could take it, doing nothing but tossing and turning from one side of the bed to the other. I kept reliving my life and knowing that life is all about choices and that sometimes there is no going backward to make changes.

I made coffee and was sitting on the couch. I wasn't sure why my mind was so unsettled, as before I came to this town it wasn't like this.

With everything that I did in my younger years, it had provided me with the money that I have today. I have had nothing but a prosperous life since I left Jenny. Yet this town, the words that Jenny spoke to me, seeing David for the first time in his life, and the coin was making me relive my past.

I knew that I had done some really bad things to get where I am today. Do I have regrets for doing them? NO, I don't. If I hadn't chosen that kind of life, I would have been struggling all these years. There were times when I did do some good things that should account for something. When I saw a homeless person holding a cup out, looking for some help, I always reached in my pocket and pulled out a bunch of money to hand to him or her. When I got tired of the clothes that I was wearing, and was ready to change styles—as I wore nothing but the best—I would take them to a shelter to give to the needy. I have given money to charitable organizations as well. This might not seem like much, but maybe what I did good might make up for some of the bad that I have done.

I have been a player and a con artist for many years, driving fancy cars, living in nothing but the best hotels or motels, and also having expensive houses in the best of neighborhoods, eating at elegant restaurants where only rich people go, and knowing that I have led a lifestyle that most people only can dream about having. Yet now I am sitting here in this luxury motel, wondering what it is that is causing me to rethink my life.

I waited until morning, and then I called a phone number that had been stuck in my brain for many years. The number belonged to Jenny's best friend, Kelly. There was a very good chance that she wouldn't even speak to me again, and if she didn't want to, who could blame her? I wanted to see if she could tell me how Jenny and David's life had gone after I walked out on them. Also, why Jenny had died.

When I dialed her number, I let the phone ring until the answering machine came on and then I left a message.

"I'm not sure if I have called the right number. It has been many years since I have spoken to a lady by the name of Kelly that had this number. If I have reached Kelly, this is Robert and I would like to speak with you if I can. Call me back on the phone number showing on your phone, and leave a message if I don't answer. I would like to talk to you again, if this is possible. Thanks."

I sat and waited for a couple more hours, drinking more coffee, waiting to see if the motel phone would ring. It didn't and I still had more parts of the town that I wanted to explore. I was thinking about either settling down here now, or just buying property for when or if I ever wanted to.

It was time to leave and again I left the coin on the dresser. Before I drove away, once again my mind took me back to what transpired after I gave up the scam of being a Stock Market broker.

For several months, after I had changed my appearance wearing clothes that I hoped I wasn't found dead in, along with an itchy beard, colored hair, fake glasses and also using a cane. Newark, being a huge city and there being no paper trail leading to me on any of the scams that I had pulled off, I felt like I might be in the clear now and could go back to the way I was before, but just for reassurance, I continued to keep my appearance the way it was at that time.

I was bored even with all of my money in the bank, and I had been to the race track several times. It seemed like every time I went, the horses that I had bet on won and I walked away with more money to add to my wallet. I was on a lucky streak, and continued to bet on the horses for months.

Knowing that I had this to fall back on, I wanted to go onto something else for entertainment, and also something to increase the money that was in my bank account as greed was the only thing I knew, and being a player I would take a chance of losing a little money if it came to that. The way my luck and life was going, my ego was needing some kind of excitement as well. The race track wasn't giving me that high that I needed any longer.

I knew where I was going next.

Before I got the job at Russ-A-Thon, when I was living at the dingy motel in a bad part of Newark, I had gotten acquainted with a couple of shifty guys that were trainers for boxers. They had been in the business of doing this for many years, and they made money of their own off of a boxing match. It all depends on who a person supports and who they don't. So that day I went back to the bad part of Newark to the place where Dan and Mike went each day to train young men and show them the ropes of how to win a fight.

When I walked through the door to the gym, where many boxers were sparring with another boxer, I saw Dan and Mike standing there talking. They glanced over at me, but with the change in my appearance, I was sure that they wouldn't know who I was.

I walked over to them and said, "Hey Dan, and Mike. Do you remember me?"

"No, sorry, bud. I don't know who you are," Dan replied as Mike stood there, shaking his head no as well.

I had fooled both of them and I wanted to laugh as there was a part of me that thought that they would see right through me and remember me just from the sound of my voice.

"It's me, guys! I'm Robby. Surely you remember me!" I said.

"No, you can't be Robby. He would never dress like you do and he sure didn't look like you," Dan replied.

"I'm being serious, guys. It *is* me," I commented.

"Come on now! This joke is getting old and you can't be Robby. If you *are* Robby, where did I last see you?" Mike asked.

"At the dingy motel that I lived in for some time when I was trying to find a job. I had just walked out of my motel room and I saw you laughing and carrying on with some blond-headed woman as you were trying to help her into your car. She had too much to drink and was laughing so hard that I thought she would wake up everyone in the motel," I said.

"It *is* you, Robby! Why are you dressed like that, and here at this place?" Mike asked.

"Let's just say that I needed to change my look and this is what you see. The reason why I am here is because I have done fairly well since the dingy motel room and would like to invest in a couple of good boxers. By the way, Mike, how did it turn out that night with the blond, and did your wife ever find out about what you were doing in the motel room?" I commented.

"Let's just say that I am single now, and as for the blond, she turned out to be a married woman, and from what I heard from other people that know her, it didn't turn out good for her either. If you are really serious about throwing money our way Robby, we are willing to take it. I didn't know that you had that kind of money to toss around on a hunch," Mike replied.

"I have made some money the last few years, and now I want to see if you two can make more for me. I know what I am doing, if I do decide to hand over cash to you both, with the understanding that I am going to double it. Before I shake hands on this deal, I need to see the boxers and watch them in action. Without this, I walk away with my money still in my pocket," I said.

"We have some young ones, Robby, and they are so far doing good for now, until they get cocky and think that they are the best. At that point if they don't change, they will be out of the ring, and the door. If you want, we can take you to the ring right now, to watch them work out. From there you can decide if you want to invest any of your money in them or even bet on them before the fight," Dan said.

I agreed that was what I needed to do and we walked away as I watched each one of the boxers in the big gym spar with a partner. I was a con and didn't want to get conned myself, so I had to be careful!

From what I could see, they looked good in the ring. Both of the boxers were young and strong. I had told Mike and Dan that I would see them tonight after the fight. If I liked what I saw, they would have money in their pockets. I would have money in mine from the investment.

That night I heard many cheers when each one of them entered the ring. They were liked by the crowd of people that came to see them. This said something to me, but I wasn't completely sure. I kept watching—not just them, but other boxers. It looked like the older boxers were losing steam. It wouldn't be long and they would be hanging up their gloves.

These two that I had picked were full of life and had won their matches before the third round. I was ready to shake hands and close the deal. I reminded both Mike, and

Dan that I was doing this to make more money than what I had handed them and that I wouldn't be happy if they didn't make it happen. After all, I was the con artist. I would make sure that I came out a winner no matter what I had to do!

Every day I would return to the gym to watch the two boxers that I had put my faith into who were making me more money right and left. With each fight I had bet money on them, confident that they would win their match. Every time they came out on top as the winners.

Dan and Mike were also raking in the dough. It looked like the boxers were on their way to the top.

I was a player during the day, and also a player at night while going to all the clubs to hang out with only the rich and famous people in Newark. When I left the clubs, I went to the ring to watch my boxers fight until the finish of the fight. My life was back on track and going even better than before. Being a loner really paid off for me as I was living my life on my terms and doing whatever I chose to do.

At the time I remember thinking how I wouldn't be where I am today with a wife nagging me and a kid strapped to me all the time. I kept thinking how the choices that I had made were going well and were only going to get better.

I continued to watch my boxers go further up the ladder, and Dan, Mike and I were still making money.

Finally, the day came when I got a call from Dan, who explained that one of our boxers was in critical condition in the hospital as he was involved in a serious accident. He almost died and he'd had several surgeries just to keep his legs. He was told by the doctor that his boxing career was over. When I went to see him, he said he was sorry for letting me down and that he had not only let me down, but also his wife and kids. With him not being able to box any longer, he wasn't sure how they were going to be able to live.

At that time, I pulled out my checkbook. I wrote him a check for $ 400,000. I felt like he had earned it. From what I could see, he would be fortunate to even walk at all. I also told him that I would take care of his hospital bills and not to worry about them. He told me that he didn't know how to thank me. I told him that when he got out of the hospital, to always make good choices in life, and that would be thanks enough for me. I had made tons of money off of each fight that he had, and what I had given him was nothing compared to what he had given to me.

The next day I went to the gym to talk to Mike and Dan. I told them that I was done with the deal and that they were on their own now. I had places to go and more conning to do. It was time again to walk away. Of course, they were fine with this as they had, like I said, made tons of money too. The boxers had made a name for themselves except for the one that almost ended his life.

We shook hands and I told them that if they were ever in the rich part of Newark to look me up. The truth is they wouldn't be able to, but I thought I would throw in those words at the end of the conversation.

They said they would. I turned around and walked out the same door that I had walked into almost three years ago. My time with the boxing scene was over and now it was time to move on to something else. Once again, my memories of the past kept flooding back to me.

As I sat in my car after thinking about my short bout with the boxers and all the excitement that went with it, I kept thinking that my life had gotten better with what I had done. I actually wanted to pat myself on the back for the way that I had helped the young man that day in the hospital. This was, I know, the most decent thing that I had ever done in my life. Once again, I had no regrets from helping him and doing this.

It wouldn't be long before I had either found what I was looking for in this small town or I would get into my car to drive to another town to look around. Later that day, when I went back to the motel, I would see if Kelly had called me back. If so, it would be interesting to meet with her, to see what had taken place all the years prior to Jenny passing away.

I kept driving around and I did find some property that I liked. I had the money to buy it and decided that if I still wanted to settle down in this area in a couple of days, I would go to the Realtor that was listed on the sign sitting in the yard, and see if I could look at the property better. If it turned out to be what I thought it was, I would buy it and try living here. I could always move somewhere else if things changed for me.

I was kind of excited to go back to the motel as I wanted to check the answering machine, to see if Kelly had responded back to me. I knew that she had to know things weren't the best between Jenny and me, and maybe there might be something inside her that had changed over the many years, and she had learned how to forgive me. Then again, maybe not?

The first place I looked when I entered my motel room was the answering machine. I could see that the light wasn't blinking, which let me know that there wasn't a message for me. Many thoughts entered my mind. Maybe Kelly was working and hadn't gotten the message yet. She might be out of town and wouldn't hear the message until she returned home. Maybe she didn't want to talk to me. Maybe the phone number that I had called wasn't hers any longer and she had moved to another place or town. Maybe she had passed away like Jenny had. I had so much speculation going on in my mind.

I sat down on the couch, once again drinking coffee and watching the phone, as if I expected it to ring any time now. Finally, I got up and decided to take a shower. If the phone did ring and it was Kelly, it would be interesting to see if she would leave me a message.

I was in the process of emptying out my pockets when once again I pulled out the flashing coin that I had left on the dresser that morning before leaving. My mind was so consumed with wondering if Kelly had called me back when I first entered my room earlier that I didn't even think about looking on the dresser to see if the coin was still there. There was no way of getting rid of it as it would just return to me, no matter what I did with it or where I put it.

Some people would refer to it as being like an arrowhead that a person finds laying on the ground. Some people believe that an arrowhead is a sign of good luck, and when a person finds one, it stays with them and is theirs until the reason why they found it either happens or goes away. The coin still continued to flash. I had to be content with this as it was a mystery and one that was unsolved for now.

I emptied the rest of my pockets on the dresser and went in the bathroom to shower. When I was finished and came back into the room, I could see that no one had tried to call me. I sat back down on the couch to drink more coffee for a while, to give Kelly a chance to get a hold of me.

When this didn't happen once again, I put everything back in my pocket of clean clothes that I had changed into, and left to go get something to eat for dinner. Tonight, my plans were to go to a small diner that I had passed today on my way back to the motel.

I hadn't seen any elegant restaurants in this town, unlike Newark. Every night I ate at a different one, where only the rich and famous went to eat out. Maybe this was a good thing and my life was changing in that respect. I wasn't ready for change as I had loved my lifestyle for years. I had no regrets on anything that I did to get to the top of the mountain that I had struggled to climb after I left Jenny.

As I sat in the diner, I was looking around at the people that came in and left. While doing this, I glanced over at a young man who was also in there. At the time, the only thing I could see was the back of his head. When the young man turned his head to look at the woman that he was with, I could see that it was David. There was also a very small child sitting there with them.

At that moment, I wanted to walk over to him and start talking, and then I stopped myself. I was the last person that David would want to see and talk to. There was no way that he would introduce me to the woman and child that were sitting with him at the table. Besides I had no regrets for what I had done. There was no point in making it look like I did.

It wasn't long and David left. I sat there, drinking my coffee and thinking back once more on my younger years, when I was at the top of my game and thought that life was my oyster.

After the wanting to be involved with the boxing crowd, I was ready to try to get back into the workforce again. I didn't really need to at that time, but a con is a con, and I felt like I needed the rush that came with doing this.

During my time of living in Newark I had met many rich people, most of whom had businesses and success. I had tried the Russ-A-Thon business and was making money hands over fist until I got fired.

My life could have gone bad for me at that time, but there was another business that I knew of that needed a CEO. I was certain that the owner, Mr. Heatherton, would still remember me. I had seen from the paper that they were looking for someone. I was sure that with this came the big bucks for whomever he chose to hire.

That night, when I returned home, I called Sam and left him a message, telling him who I was, and that I might be his man that could make him more money. Also, I gave him my phone number from the phone that I did have at that time. The other phones that I had in the past had been destroyed after a while. This way, no one would be able to talk to me unless I wanted them to.

I was bored and needed more entertainment in my life, even if it meant returning to a job every day. Also fattening my wallet and bank account was a plus.

I went to bed, and the next morning I was awakened by the phone ringing. I let whomever it was calling leave me a message. This is what I heard.

"Robert, this is Mr. Heatherton from Heatherton Industries. I got your message late last night. I didn't want to disturb you, for fear that you would be sleeping. I do have an opening available right now. I would be happy to speak to you about this. When you get this message, give me a call and we can talk about a good appointment time when I can meet with you."

I had done it. At least I believed that I had. I was very confident that I would get the job. After I got the layout of the business, I would see if I was going to be able to pull off maybe another con or if not, I would walk away without making myself richer. That would be the only way that I would take any job from now on. I loved playing people. There was no way that they could ever be able to play me. That is the way good con artists roll.

As I grew up, I used to be a nice, trusting person whom everyone could trust, but it didn't take me long to realize that nice guys finish last. Knowing who to trust is like a game of cards. It's hard to know what the other person has by the look on his or her face. This is because they are good at the game. You either trust them, or trust yourself and put on your game face in life.

This is when I learned how to be a con artist and a player. Every day I put on the best game face that I have.

—4—

LIVING THE WRONG LIFE

That morning I did call Mr. Heatherton back again. He had a meeting with his board of directors later in the morning. He had told me to be at his office at 1:00 p.m.

I arrived a little early that day, to make it look good, and was waiting inside a room where his receptionist was. I was ready to sell myself to him with the usual line of how I would be the best man for the job and the man that he needed to be his CEO of his company. Within an hour, Mr. Heatherton walked through the door. He saw me waiting for him and walked over to me.

"Robert, it is good to see you again. I believe the last time I saw you was at Russ-A-Thon," he said.

"It's nice to see you once again as well. Thank you for returning my phone call to you," I replied as we shook hands. He told me to follow him into his office and we sat down at his desk.

"Tell me, Robert, why do you believe that you will be able to be an asset to my company?" he asked.

"I have been a business man for many years, Mr. Heatherton, even before I came to Newark. I am reliable, honest, on time every day, and I have made money for many companies along the way that I have worked for. Being a hard worker, I find many ways to make huge amounts of money for the company and increase their sales. Basically, there isn't anything that I can't do," I replied.

"If I did choose you for this job, you would be the CEO of my fashion house. I have many designers that I rely on each day to create a new style for thousands of people. You would be dealing with them every day. There is a lot of competition in this industry, Robert. The job would be very time consuming. It would require you reaching out to many people and companies that will take their business elsewhere if we aren't on top of it all the time.

"I know that you have worked in business before. This job is, I am sure, something that you haven't done before. If I hire you, I will pay you well as this is what I do, but with that I expect a lot from you as well. Now that you know more about what you are dealing with working here, do you think that you can handle this kind of work?" he asked.

"You are right, Mr. Heatherton. I haven't worked with fashion before, but I do know how to promote products, no matter what they are. I don't have a problem working extra hours if this is what it takes for me to get the job done and done right. It won't take me long to learn the business here, and at the end of the day you will be able to go home and relax because you will have the reassurance that I am in control," I responded.

"Then, Robert, I am going to give you a chance to prove yourself to me. You will see that I am a tough boss to please, so I will be in and out of the office quite frequently. Welcome on board with Heatherton Industries," he remarked.

"I won't let you down. I will see to it that you get everything that you have coming to you and more," I said.

"Now that you are working for me, call me Sam," he said as he shook my hand.

I had looked Sam in the eyes the entire time we were talking. My words were convincing and my mannerism was just what he was looking for. I was sincere, point blank and with sincerity I had sold myself. In reality, the only person that I was in that job for was myself. If this meant helping myself to some of his money, then so be it.

We had agreed that tomorrow morning I would start work for him, bright and early at 9:00 a.m. I once again shook his hand and told him thank you for the job. I turned around and walked out of his office. I was confident that there was going to be something in this for me.

On the way back to my penthouse, I stopped at a library to do some research on what I was going to be doing as he was right, I hadn't done this work before. I had no clue about what all a fashion house did or how it all worked. I spent a couple of hours in the library, researching his business, what type of fashion they designed, and how everything operated. I felt confident that I was prepared for what all I was dealing with, and what I could gain for myself.

My idea was to make sure that his name brand clothing not only was headed to the right places for sale, but also that there would be something in it for me as well. I was sure that I could take the clothing scanning tags that were from this company and also include ones that were similar that would be from my fake company.

If things went bad, it wouldn't be my fault as I wasn't the one putting the scanning tags on the clothes or even making them. I just had to find someone that would make the scanning tags with numbers on them to include with the real ones. I would make sure *my* tags were with the employees that worked there and did this for a living. This shouldn't be too hard as the employees that did this wouldn't be able to tell the difference. They would have no idea that the numbers on the scanning tags were different than the ones that they had been putting on the clothes for years.

I would once again have a fake ID to create a bank account and phone number with a fake company name that would actually belong to me that would be connected with a knock-off shop. No one would be the wiser as all of these styles of different clothing were being distributed to many stores all over the country.

I felt like I was in charge again, and that I would be

playing the part of a decent CEO doing this job every day, with no one being the wiser. I would be making money hand over fist again with a self-made fake company with my seal of approval on the tags attached.

I had this plan all worked out in my head. Now I had to find the right place that would design and create the fake tags that I was going to use, or should I say the employees working in that department in the company would use as they attached them to the clothes.

I would know soon enough once the tags were in the right place if my plan would be noticed right away. I was the new man working there and the last one that anyone would suspect.

I went to work every day and got the feel for the job. I had seen Mr. Heatherton many times. He seemed impressed that I was learning my job as quickly as I was. I had found a place that was located out of state that was more than willing to create the fake tags for a hefty price, which I would provide them with. So now everything was in place and ready to go. The knock-off tags were mixed in with the actual designer ones. Unless the person attaching them on the clothing looked, I was set to jet.

I had walked all over the company and everyone was busy doing their jobs. I even walked down to where the tags were being put on by hand, getting each item ready for shipment. No one as of yet bothered to look at them. They were so similar that even if they did, my guess was that they wouldn't notice the difference. Soon the clothing would be ready. Then it would be awhile before I checked my bank to see if any money had been deposited. If it had, I would know that my plan had worked.

With me knowing that there was a high demand for designer clothing and many companies that continued to be in competition I wasn't expecting to see any amount in the bank for a while. This con with Heatherton Industries was a test to see if what I was trying to pull off was going to work out the way that I thought that it would. If it didn't, I would eventually move on to something else. A good con artist takes his time, and doesn't try to rush anything as there is always that chance of something bad that could happen.

Each week I received a nice paycheck from Mr. Heatherton. He wasn't kidding me when he said that he paid well. I continued to pretend to be the smiling, hardworking employee that walked around, looking and making sure that everything was running smoothly within the company.

This went on for weeks. Even months had passed since I first started my new job. I decided that I had given it enough time, and that it was time for me to go to the bank to see if there was any amount that had been deposited. When I talked to the lady cashier, I was informed that there had been a check deposited in the amount of $120,000 the day before yesterday. At that time, I knew for sure that the con had worked. Once again, I was on my way to becoming a richer man.

I left the bank and returned to work with an even bigger smile on my face. The next thing that I needed to make sure of was that the company was also making plenty of money still, or Mr. Heatherton would know that something was wrong and start having someone investigate the layout of the company, to see why the business was no longer making the good money that they had made in the past.

That afternoon there was a board meeting. I had been asked to attend. This could be a good thing or a bad thing, depending on the discussion that would take place in that room today.

As I walked into the room that afternoon, I didn't know what to expect ... BUT .... I entered it looking confident, and once again wearing a big smile. Being prepared for anything, I sat down in one chair of many that were around a big table, where Mr. Heatherton sat at the end, so that he could watch all of us in there and talk directly to everyone that he had chosen to be there that day. He started the board meeting. This was what was said:

"I'm glad that all of you were able to fit this meeting

into your busy schedules. It has been a few months since I have called all of you in here. Today as we always do, we will be discussing the productivity of the company, and see if any changes are suggested. Before we get to the increase or decrease of sales, I want to know if any of you would like to make or share with the rest of us any suggestion or a question directed at me?" Mr. Heatherton said.

"I have one," Henry Jones, the head of marketing, said.

"Okay, Henry. Let's hear what you would like to say."

"This might not be of that great of importance to add to this meeting, but I would like to bring up to you the possibility of putting in place more coffee machines throughout the company. The reason why I am asking this is because not all of the workers take a break at the same time. The employees that work on the bottom floor have complained to me about this. Apparently, when they take their breaks, the coffee is gone and no one has bothered to make more of it. The coffee makers are on the second floor, and with a 20-minute break they are rushed getting to the coffee machines and then making it back to where they work on time. With the job that they do, they feel that the coffee helps them to keep motivated with their work," Henry replied.

"This is a good request, Henry. I am sure that I can have more coffee machines installed throughout the company to make the workers happy, so that they, too, get their fair share," Mr. Heatherton commented.

"I too have a question for you, Sam," Bill Worthy, the head of distribution said.

"I'm happy to see you participating in this meeting, Bill. In the last one you were very quiet and you looked distracted. I wasn't sure if you were even paying attention to what was said in here," Mr. Heatherton spoke.

"At that time, Sam, I was having some personal problems that I needed to take care of. Everything is fine now. As you can see, I am sitting here ready to discuss whatever we need to. My suggestion that I have for you today is this. The trucks that come here to pick up the boxes that we ship with have been allowed to leave their big trucks parked on the employee parking lot overnight if they finish loading late, and need to stay over until morning. Because of this, some of the trucks have blocked employees in their parking spots where their vehicle has to sit the entire night. Our workers are then forced into finding a ride home from either another employee, or someone else. If this had only happened once or twice, I wouldn't be bringing it up now, but this has been going on for some time now. Some of the employees are saying that they feel like they need to find another job as they don't like leaving their vehicles unattended, or needing to look for a ride after they have put in a full day of work," Bill replied.

"Bill, I can see the dilemma that the workers are having. As you know, I am a company man that wants to make everyone who works here happy and feeling good about their job, and the company. I will speak to the company that we have contracted the trucks through, to see if we can't come up with a solution on how to solve this. Hopefully, they can park in a nearby parking lot somewhere else. This was a good request. I'm glad that everything is going good with you now, and that you participated here today," Mr. Heatherton responded.

"I too have a question," Tom Parks, head of the design department, said.

"What is it that you want to know, Tom?"

"Models that we have hired and use for our fashion shows are asking if you will furnish them with a larger room where they can get ready before the fashion shows start. They are complaining about not having enough room and running into each other in the process of getting dressed."

"I don't think that this is an unreasonable request, Tom. I will see that they now have a larger room to get ready in from now on. If the models don't look good when they walk down the runway, then it doesn't look good for us. Are there any more questions that you would like to ask or suggestions? If not, I would like to get to the productivity report," Mr. Heatherton said.

This was what I wanted to hear! I really didn't care about all of the whining employees that felt like their life was ruined because of no coffee, needing to leave their cars, or models that were spoiled and wanted the largest room in the building to dress in and put makeup on or personal problems. My focus was on whether Mr. Heatherton said that the sales were down or increasing. I still continued to sit there with a stupid big smile on my face, making it look like I really cared about all the dumb questions and suggestions. I just sat there waiting to hear what was said

"I know that you are waiting patiently for me to tell you how the last months of productivity have been. I will get right into it. From what I am seeing, it looks like our sales are staying the same in some areas and doing better in others. I am hoping that the next report is a better one, but the company is still making money. We will have another board meeting in a couple of months. At that time, I will let you know how things are going and if anything has changed. Go back to work now as the meeting is over," Mr. Heatherton instructed.

I was so happy, I wanted to jump up and down in my chair. Instead, I had to look professional and act like the other stuffed shirts in the meeting. I got up from my chair and shook Mr. Heatherton's hand. I told him that I appreciated being included in the meeting and that, if possible, I would like to attend all of them. I also told him that I was very impressed with the suggestions that were made. I also told him that this was the first board meeting that I had attended in my years of being a business man. He assured me that I would be included with all of them, and if I, too, had a question or a suggestion, to feel free to ask or give my input on whatever I had on my mind.

If he only knew what I went there today to find out, he would have tossed me out on my ear, or worse. I thanked him and turned around to walk away. It looked like, for now, no one was the wiser and that my con was working.

That day I stayed at the company for a few hours longer, to make it look good. Then I decided to try a different restaurant that night. This one was closer to the outskirts of Newark, where no one but the rich people went to.

I was escorted to my chair with a menu placed in front of me. I happened to glance at the door. I saw a man that I hadn't seen for many years. He had seen me come in and waited until I was alone before coming over to my table.

"Hello, Robert. What brings you to the outskirts of Newark tonight other than eating here?" a man called Steve Andrews asked.

"Nothing really, Steve, other than wanting to try out a different restaurant, which is what I try to do each night. It has been years since I saw you. I hope that everything is going good with you and your family," I responded.

"Everything is going fabulous, Robert. I am still working for the same company that I was working for years ago. My wife and I are very happy. My niece, Taylor, is flying in from Chicago tomorrow. She will be staying with us for a while. She has never been here before. We are very excited to see her again and spend time with her. She has been working and living in Chicago for some time and needed some time away for now," Steve spoke.

"This sounds exciting for you and your wife, Steve. I hope that the visit with her goes well for all of you," I said.

"I am sure that it will. I have an idea, Robert, if you are interested. My wife and I are having a dinner party tomorrow night at 8:00. We would love for you to come to it, if you have the time," Steve said.

"I would love to come over to your home for this, Steve. Thank you for including me in this. I will need your address, and 8:00 will work perfectly for me," I responded as Steve wrote down his address for me.

"Then it's a plan, Robert. If you want, you can come over a little early. We can have a drink before the others arrive," Steve said.

"I don't drink, Steve, but I would love to come over a

little early. I will see you tomorrow night," I spoke.

"That sounds good and I will see you when you arrive," Steve said just before he walked away.

I wasn't much into dinner parties, but with dinner parties comes more rich people to get acquainted with, and a free meal. Who knows, this get-together might pay off for later on down the road for me? I had ordered and soon after, they were bringing me my food. I ate and was ready to leave to go back to my penthouse for hopefully a good night of sleep.

In the morning after a shower and some coffee, I was on my way to the office. I had called my bank. Another deposit in the amount of $50,000 was showing in my account. I was really starting to rake in the dough. This was the whole idea. Someday I would have more money than I would know what to do with and a lot of memories of how I got it.

After arriving at the office, I did what I did every day. I walked around the company, checking to make sure that all of the workers were still doing their jobs. This was important as I knew that if they weren't, it would affect me as well.

Mr. Heatherton had already started the process of having more coffee machines installed throughout the entire building. This would put a stop to the sniveling employees that used the excuse of needing coffee in order to do their job. I had also noticed that there were no tractor trailer rigs parked in the parking lot. I was sure that the company that employed the truck drivers that picked up the shipments from here must have already been contacted and told that if it got late after they had loaded their trucks, to park their trucks elsewhere. This, too, would stop the whining of the workers that had threatened to leave the company and work somewhere else. As for the models' request of needing a larger room to get ready in before the fashion show, I was sure that Mr. Heatherton had taken care of this matter as well.

Everything was running smoothly, so I returned to my office to pass the day before leaving to return to my penthouse to stay until time for me to get ready for the dinner party.

I had checked out all of the inventory that was ready to ship and given my receptionist the inventory sheet. I informed her that I was leaving for the day. At that time, she was busy on the phone, speaking to several people either about their orders, or taking more. From there, I went home to sit and wait until it was time to get ready for the dinner party.

At 6:30 p.m. I left. I was sure that by showing up at the house a half hour early, before time for the other guests to arrive, would be acceptable.

It took me an hour to drive through heavy traffic to get to Steve's home on the hill, where all the other rich people lived. He had a valet standing in the long circle drive, waiting to park my car for me. This looked to me as if there were many guests that would be arriving for a huge shindig.

After I had walked to the front door and rung the doorbell, another man opened the door. I announced who I was. He had a list of the names of the guests. When he saw my name included on it, he told me to come in.

When I entered, Steve saw me and invited me over to introduce me to his niece and wife.

"Robert, I am so glad that you came early tonight. I was hoping that you would. I want you to meet my wife, Nikki, and my niece, Taylor," Steve spoke.

Taylor was standing and talking to Nikki at the time when Steve and I walked over to them. We approached them and they turned around.

"Nikki, Taylor, this is Robert Stone. He is the CEO I have told you about."

Nikki extended her hand to shake mine and Taylor did the same thing. I felt like I was in a palace with not just one, but two beautiful princesses standing in front of me.

"Robert, it is very nice to meet you. I am happy that you could join us tonight," Nikki commented.

"I am pleased to meet you as well," Taylor spoke.

"My thanks are extended to you both, Nikki and Steve,

for inviting me to join you in your beautiful home for your dinner party," I replied.

At that moment, the doorbell rang and more people had also decided to arrive early. This was going to be an adventurous night for me to meet more important people that might benefit my lifestyle later, if I chose them to.

When Steve and Nikki walked away, Taylor continued to stand where she was. She was not only beautiful, but was wearing an exquisite dress that looked like it was one that Heatherton Industries had designed. I continued to talk to her.

"So, Taylor, Steve told me that you come from Chicago. I haven't been to that city as of yet, but I have heard many things about it. I know that you haven't had time to see any of Newark as you just arrived here. If you would like, I would be happy to show you around some," I spoke.

"That would be nice of you to do this for me. I am planning on staying for a few weeks. I know that my uncle and aunt will be busy working most of the time. I have been wondering how I would see the city with me not being familiar with any of the sights here," Taylor responded.

"Before I leave tonight, I will give you my phone number. Anytime that you want to see the sights, give me a call. I will drive you around," I said as I looked into her eyes.

At that time, Steve had brought another man and woman over to meet Taylor and me. This continued to happen until the maid announced that we were to go to the main dining room as dinner would be served shortly. I followed Taylor and Steve in there. The table that we were to sit at was about as big as one of my rooms in my penthouse. It was filled with very expensive china. When we sat down, I sat next to Taylor.

Everyone was being served and the glasses were filled. There was a toast to Nikki and Steve for inviting all of us there. Then the plates were filled with wonderful cuisine that was placed in front of us. As everyone ate, I recognized some of the guests that had attended as being businessmen that had visited Russ-A-Thon from time to time. None of them remembered me. This was probably a good thing. During the dinner there was a lot of talking, and I was trying to listen to every conversation.

When we had finished eating, we all got up from the table and returned to the main room in the house for beverages and conversation. I continued to watch and listen to everyone who was there. At times I would approach one of the guests and join in. I wanted to remember their names and hopefully they would remember mine.

I noticed that Taylor continued to glance over at me once in a while with a smile. She was busy as Steve and Nikki had her speaking to all of the guests as well. They wanted to make sure that she had a good time at the party and got acquainted with everyone and not just me. When she did smile at me, I smiled back.

As the night progressed, everyone was announcing that it was late and they would be leaving. Also, they were shaking Steve's, Nikki's and Taylor's hands, telling them that the dinner party was wonderful and that they would see them soon at maybe a dinner party that they would have. I was the last guest still remaining.

"Robert, it looks like all of the others have left. Would you like another beverage and we can talk for a while longer?" Steve asked.

"I have a very early appointment in the morning, Steve, and it is late. I think I will take a rain check on the other beverage for another time. Thank you both for inviting me. You both are very gracious people, and Taylor, it was very nice to meet you. When you are ready, give me a call. I will be happy to give you a tour of the city," I spoke as I handed Taylor my phone number.

"Thank you for coming, Robert. Have a safe drive home. I am sure that we will see you soon," Steve spoke as he shook my hand.

I left and it was around midnight before I walked through my front door. I had met several important people tonight that I felt were impressed with me. If need be, I would know where to go for whatever I needed to use them for.

Before I left to go to work the next day, I checked my bank account once again. This time there were no new deposits made. I wasn't surprised. If I was the only one getting all the money from sales in my account and not money also being deposited in the account for Heatherton Industries, it wouldn't be long and I would be looking for a new job as the company would need to go bankrupt or there would be an investigation throughout the entire company. I wasn't willing to take it that far. There would be a time when I would be quitting my job and getting out of it while I still could.

When I told Steve, Nikki and Taylor that I had an early appointment and that I needed to leave, I wasn't being honest with them. It was an excuse that I made because I was afraid that Steve would ask questions that I didn't want to answer. One being, if I still worked for Russ-A-Thon. I didn't tell him that I had gotten fired and the company that I now was working for. A good con artist knows that it is best, if possible, to keep some things being directed at him or her short, sweet and believable when it comes to many things.

The truth was that today I didn't even need to go to work if I chose not to, but because I still wanted to look like the hard-working, early-to-work guy, I would make an appearance for a short time, just to once again walk around the company and check out how the workers were doing.

When I arrived at work, everything was still going well. I told my receptionist that I had things I had to take care of, and would see her in the morning. I left the building and went to the track to do some betting on some horses. Once again, my horses that I picked did well. I walked away with more money than I had spent that day.

After I arrived home, my cell phone rang. The call was coming from a number that I didn't recognize. I let my voicemail get the message. When I checked the voicemail, I saw that Taylor was the caller. I waited a short time and then I called the number back. The message that was left said, "Hello, this is Taylor calling. I thought I would give you a call to let you know that if it works for you and your schedule, that my calendar is empty for now. I can meet with you anytime. When you can, give me a call back if you want," Taylor had said.

I did call Taylor back and it rang a couple of times before she answered.

"Hello," Taylor said.

"I was happy to hear from you, Taylor. I will be booked up until Saturday. Will this work for you?" I asked.

"Yes, Robert, that would be fine. Now that you have my number, give me a call on the time that you would like to pick me up," she commented.

"I will check my calendar and then get back to you with a time when I will be arriving at Steve's house," I responded.

"That works and thank you, Robert, as I am curious to know what Newark is all about," Taylor said.

I told her that I would get back to her with a time later that evening as I didn't want to look too eager with telling her a time at that moment. The truth be known, anytime would have worked for me on Saturday as I had nothing important planned for that day.

The next day at work, I waited until late afternoon until I called her back. At that time, I told Taylor that I could pick her up at 11:00 a.m. and, depending on the traffic flow within the city, I would like to take her to a nice restaurant for lunch before I showed her parts of Newark. I also explained that it might take more than one outing of sightseeing for her to see everything that was worth seeing. Taylor agreed that everything sounded good to her. She told me that she would be ready when I arrived. So, it was a date planned.

The rest of my work week went by fairly quickly. I did my normal things that I did every day and finally it was the beginning of the weekend. I didn't have any friends in Newark, just acquaintances. I liked it that way. In fact, I didn't think I had any friends anywhere now. There were many pluses to this as no one other than me knew my business. Because I didn't know theirs, I was much happier. The only one I worried about was me.

That morning I had gotten ready to leave my home to pick up Taylor and show her as much of the city as I could. I had lived in Newark for 22 years. I was sure there were many things that I had driven past and didn't even take the time to look at. This time with Taylor and seeing the sights might turn out to be an adventure for me as well.

I left the house at 9:30 a.m. to give myself extra time to get to Steve's home. I was glad that I did as the traffic once again was horrible, like it always was on the weekend.

When I arrived at Steve's home, I was a little early, but Taylor was ready to go like she said that she would be. From there, we drove to a very nice restaurant. My mind was always working. If I made Steve's niece happy, there might come a time when I needed a favor from Steve and then I could play that card to get what I wanted. Then again, she wasn't bad to look at, so this was a plus in itself.

As we were in the car, we started talking some about different things.

"I hope that you enjoy your day out today, Taylor. I am going to try to make it as enjoyable as I can for you," I spoke.

"Robert, I am sure that I will have a lot of fun. I know that my aunt and uncle are very busy like you are and would take me to see some of the sights. To be honest, Robert, I think that seeing the city with you will be very enjoyable."

"Thank you, Taylor. I hope I live up to your expectations," I said as we arrived at the nice restaurant.

Like a gentleman, I got out of the car and went to open the car door for Taylor. This made her smile again.

We laughed as we ate. When we were done eating lunch, we were on our way to see the Cathedral Basilica of the Heart. After that, I would be taking her to see the Yankee Stadium. She told me that she wanted to go there her whole life. Next on the list of adventure spots was the Princeton University. There was so much to see and I knew that we couldn't see it all in one day.

Around 7:00 p.m. I asked Taylor if she wanted to go out to another nice restaurant to eat dinner. I told her the name of the restaurant and that I had last seen her Uncle Steve there when he invited me to the dinner party. In my opinion, it was on the top of the list for elegance, and of course she said that she would love to stop there and eat.

During dinner, once again we talked about small things. She didn't ask me any personal questions as I didn't her. We had fun that day. When we were finished eating, it was late and time to take her home.

"Robert, thank you so much for taking me to some of the beautiful sights today that I saw. It means a lot to me," Taylor said.

"My pleasure, Taylor. There are many sights here that I haven't seen either, so we are seeing them together for the first time. If you would like, I can pick you up tomorrow for another day of fun and show you more of Newark and what it offers," I replied.

"I would love it! What time should I expect you at the house?" Taylor asked.

"I think we should get an earlier start, if that is okay with you. Instead of taking you to eat lunch, I would like to take you out to breakfast. From there we will have the whole day to explore the city," I commented.

"That would be wonderful and again thank you!" Taylor replied.

"If it is okay with you, I should be at the house at 9:00," I responded.

By then, we had arrived back at Steve and Nikki's home and once again I got out of the car to walk around to the other side of my car to open the door for her. This made her smile once again. I walked her to the door and told her that I would be there bright and early and for her to have a good night.

If Steve was in the house waiting for Taylor to return, he probably thought that I would come in and have the beverage that he offered me the other night. Maybe another day, but not that night.

—5—

WAS I RIGHT, OR WRONG?

After Taylor had entered the house, I walked back to my car to once again drive through heavy traffic to get home. Steve's house was across the city and some distance from where I was living.

It had been an interesting day. Under different circumstances, and with a different lifestyle, I might have been interested in pursuing maybe a relationship with Taylor as she was not only an interesting person to be around, but also very charming and beautiful. But there was no way that I could bring another woman into my life full time as with what Jenny had done to me had soured my taste with any woman.

The next morning I was up early as if it was a work day. I was ready for some more fun and on my way to retrieve Taylor from the house once again. Today, when I pulled up in the long circle driveway and parked in front of the house, I was preparing to get out when I saw Taylor walking toward my car. I was wondering what that was all about. I got out of the car and walked around it once again to let her in.

"Taylor, I would have gladly gone to the front door to get you," I remarked.

"I know that you would have, Robert. I just was afraid that with it being a Sunday morning, my aunt and uncle might still be sleeping in and thought that maybe it would be best if I just watched for you and met you at the car instead," Taylor replied.

"This is true, and yes, maybe it was a good thing that you chose to do this. When I gave you a time to be ready, I wasn't thinking about the fact that everyone might want to sleep in," I spoke.

"It's fine. I was awake anyway, wondering what all we are going to do today. It wasn't a big deal for me to meet you at your car," she said with a smile.

We continued to drive to another elegant restaurant that I was sure would make her happy, where she would enjoy eating breakfast. The traffic for the moment was lighter than it was yesterday. Taylor told me that she worked in a museum in Chicago, so I asked her if she would like to visit the Newark museum and look at all of the arts that they had in there. She said yes. So, this was where we were going.

After we had gone through it, we still had more time left in our day, so my next question to her was this.

"Would you like to see Six Flags? It is a fun park that I think you will enjoy."

"I would love to go there. When I was a child, my parents took me to one. At that time, I didn't have much fun. I was too short to go on a lot of the rides. It seemed boring to me, but now that I am a grown lady, I am sure that I will enjoy it very much. Thank you, Robert!" Taylor spoke.

"I am happy to be a part of taking you around Newark to show you the sights Taylor. I am also glad that you have enjoyed yourself." I responded.

While we were at Six Flags, Taylor and I shared a bag of cotton candy. While riding each ride, we were yelling and screaming like the others that were on the rides, either trying hard not to throw up or just having fun.

We were becoming friends and I wasn't sure that this was what I wanted. I had been a loner for many years, and my business and what I did was for no one to know but me.

Taylor was a sweet person. It was hard for me to keep

myself from wanting to feel something more than just being there for her to show her interesting places.

It was starting to get late in the evening and I wanted to take her to a nice place to eat dinner before I took her home. The day had gone faster than I thought it would. There were some other places that I wanted her to see. I told her that since my work week was beginning, if she wanted to see other sights of the city next Saturday, I would pick her up and show her more of what Newark had to offer.

Of course, she was in agreement. I told her that I would give her a call between now and then, to give her a time. Taylor said that it was fine with her.

We stopped and ate dinner and then once again I took her to the house and walked her to her front door. While driving back to my home, I was wondering how long it would be before Steve met us at the front door, asking me to come inside for that beverage that he wanted me to have.

As it turned out, that Monday morning when I was sitting at my desk, preparing for my day, my phone rang. It was showing Taylor as being the caller. This seemed strange to me that she would do this, but I answered my phone anyway.

"Robert, my friend, Taylor has told me how much fun she has had this past weekend. I am happy that you two have connected and that you are taking her around to see different places here," Steve said.

"Steve, I was expecting Taylor to be on the other end of this conversation. Yes, we both have enjoyed ourselves. Your niece is a very special person and fun to be around. It has been my pleasure to do this for her. It has been late both nights when we arrived at your home. I didn't want to bother either you or your lovely wife, Nikki, showing up inside the house. I assumed that both of you might have gone to bed or were planning to," I replied.

"It would have been fine if you did. On the weekend we don't go to bed early unless we have something planned for the next day. This next weekend, come in after you bring

Taylor home. We can have that beverage that I promised you. Just so you know, I am calling you from Taylor's phone because I thought that you might not recognize my phone number. I wanted to speak to you before I went to work," Steve commented.

"Okay, Steve, I understand on both counts. I will be happy to come into the house after I bring Taylor home," I replied.

"That sounds good. It will be nice to visit with you again," Steve said.

I wasn't sure what to think about any of what I had just heard from Steve. He was a nice guy, but not one that I would want as a best friend. I knew that with more interaction that I had with him, there was a good chance that he would ask me more questions. Being a con artist, I knew that before long I would be forced into either making up something, or telling him a false name of where I was working now, in case he brought up Russ-A-Thon and asked me if I was still working there. If this did happen, I would tell him a whopper of a story.

I went on with my day and did take time to call my bank to check the balance. Once again there was a new deposit for $100,000 showing. I didn't bother to ask which company the money had come from. I was making good money where I was at now, with a great paycheck each week being handed to me. Also, the benefit of my scam was going great. What else could a guy want in life?

That day I did my normal things that I always do. The rest of the work week went fairly fast once again. On Friday I called Taylor and told her that I would pick her up at 9:00 a.m. again. I also suggested that if she wanted to, she could meet me at my car. I was going to try to make this the last weekend of sightseeing. It had been fun and all, but I wasn't going to be involved with another woman again. I didn't want Taylor to think that the time that I had spent with her was leading up to a relationship.

On Saturday morning, after I retrieved her from the

house, we once again went out to eat breakfast, stopping at a restaurant that was on the way to the Bronx Zoo. If we had time after visiting the zoo, we were going to see the Branch Brook Park and walk around for a while. If things went well that day, and Taylor wanted to go, I would take her to see the Bushkill Falls on Sunday and that would be the last time I would see her. This was my plan.

We had a great time at the zoo and the park that day. As we were walking around, looking at everything that the park had to offer, Taylor grabbed hold of my hand. This took me somewhat by surprise and I didn't want to be rude. I continued to hold her hand. We continued to talk about nothing much of importance, other than occasional small talk. It was a beautiful day with the sun shining brighter than it had shone in many days.

The more we talked and the longer Taylor held my hand, the more I wanted to feel something in my heart for her. At one point I almost kissed her. This was not good. I knew that I was letting my emotions get out of control, so I let go of her hand and kept walking with her.

After we had finished with what we had planned that day, I took her back to the house. I knew that Steve was expecting me to come into his home this time for a beverage and more small talk.

When we arrived back to the house this time, we both went inside. Steve and Nikki heard the car drive up and were waiting for us to come in. Steve had remembered that I didn't drink alcohol and went to get me a glass of iced tea instead to drink while I was there. Nikki and Steve told Taylor and me to follow them into the family room, where we would all be more comfortable.

"Robert, I am happy that you took me up on coming inside to visit for a while. Here is your beverage. I am pretty sure that it is the same kind of tea that you drank the night of our party," Steve said.

"Yes, it is Steve. Thank you for inviting me here once again," I replied.

"You are always welcome here, Robert. We are pleased that you joined us tonight," Steve responded.

If all three of them knew what I really did for a living, they wouldn't want me anywhere in here, and Steve wouldn't have let Taylor leave the house with me.

"Thank you, Steve."

"Tell me, Robert, how do you still feel about working at Russ-A-Thon?" Steve asked.

Here came the personal question that I had been anticipating. I did what I knew I would need to do and that was to tell him a whopper of a story, in order to keep that question from coming up again in the near future, if there was one, should I see Steve again after tomorrow.

"Steve, I don't work for that company any longer. I have been working for a fairly new one out of New York. It is called Brandon Enterprises. It hasn't been around long, but seems to be a good place for me to work. I make decent money. I like the boss and the work hours that I have. The drive is longer for me each day, but I don't mind doing that. Someday the company might expand into Newark, but for now they are just based in New York City. They deal with supplying many places with textiles. This is why I got the job because of the many years of experience that I have working with many companies selling the same product," I replied, wondering where the nearest mirror was, so I could look to see if my nose had grown longer from all the lies that just came out of my mouth.

"That sounds like a very challenging and interesting job, Robert. I had no idea that you had left Russ-A-Thon. Of course, it has been many years since I have been inside of that company. I don't know how true the story I heard is, but I heard that after the stock market crashed, the owner, Ted Jones, was anticipating bankruptcy. I have no idea why, or if the story I heard is even true. I just assumed that you were still working there, but it sounds like you landed yourself a much better job with this other company. This one sounds like it might be more secure as well. I am anxious to hear about your venture out today, and what all you saw and did. I am sure you both had a lot of fun," Steve spoke.

"We did, Uncle Steve. I will tell you all about our day later as I am sure that Robert is tired. I'm sure he would like to return home to sleep and get ready for tomorrow as he is taking me once again to a different place in the morning," Taylor said.

"Okay, Robert, I won't keep you. Maybe you will have time to come back in the house when you return tomorrow for another beverage if you like," Steve commented.

"I will see, Steve. I have a very busy week waiting for me on Monday. I might need to bring Taylor back here earlier in the day and return to my home to prepare for my work week," I replied.

"That's fine if you can't this time, Robert. It has been nice visiting with you. Come back as often as you want," Steve spoke

"Thank you, Steve and Nikki, for your hospitality. I will see you early tomorrow morning, Taylor," I said as I got up from the couch, shaking Steve's and Nikki's hands before all three of them walked me to the front door to leave.

Taylor had given me a way out. I did appreciate this. If I had stayed in there much longer, it was hard to tell what kind of questions Steve would have asked next. There would have been more lies that I would have told to all of them.

That night, just to see if Russ-A-Thon was still in business, I drove past the building. The sign was still in place with lots of employees' cars parked in the parking lot. It looked like what Steve had heard was just a story that didn't happen.

On my drive back home, I managed to find a place where I hadn't been before. It appeared elegant on the outside, and when I went in it, I saw that it was just as elegant inside. If the food was good, I would take Taylor there to eat tomorrow morning. The food was everything that I thought it would be, so this would be the place where we ate before we started our day.

The next morning, I was ready for some fun. I had already beat the heavy traffic that occurs on Sunday morning ,which only gets worse as the day progresses. I did manage to be at Steve's house on time to get Taylor.

Once again, she was coming out of the front door when I arrived there. This would be something that I would miss after today as she was a sweet, kind, beautiful, fun and adventurous woman. I had made a friend, but I was afraid to keep seeing her as my heart was playing tricks on me. I am who I am, and won't change my ways for any woman. I couldn't subject Taylor to my kind of lifestyle. Today, when I told her goodbye, would be the last time that I would see her.

That day turned out to be amazing. We had not only gone to Bushkill Falls, but also we had gone back to the Branch Brook Park. Taylor had the cook at the house fix a lunch for us to take with us. This was her way of thanking me for all the many times that I had given my time to show her the tourist sights of Newark.

After we had walked into the park, Taylor laid out a blanket on the grass so that we could sit down and eat. In a small cooler she had fried chicken, potato salad, and pork and beans. She also remembered to bring a large container of my favorite iced tea for us to drink. Taylor had made this a special day for me as well.

When we were done eating, Taylor put the plates and what was left of the food back in the cooler. We both had eaten as much as we could without making ourselves sick. We laid back on the blanket.

Taylor decided to tell me that she had been married once before to a man whom she trusted, and that he had let her down in many ways. She said that he didn't understand her wants and needs, and didn't even try to after years of marriage. She told me that he wanted kids, but she didn't. She wanted to focus on her career.

This was a big problem for them in their marriage. He was coming home late, and spending so much time at work that they never did anything or went anywhere. He kept treating her like she didn't matter to him because her thoughts were different than his. The only thing that she felt was left for her to do was to file for a divorce. After it was finalized, she left her home and moved to Chicago, where she got a job with the museum.

Taylor's story sounded similar to mine, even though mine was a little harsher than hers. But it appeared that we did have some things in common.

I was still feeling something inside for her that I hadn't felt in 21 years. My instinct was telling me to give it a chance. If she was interested, I was ready to tell her about Jenny and my relationship that I, too, had walked away from. If it did turn into something more with Taylor, we could have fun in life with maybe traveling at times to see more sights that we hadn't seen.

As for being totally honest with her on what I had done after I left Jenny, and what I had done in order to gain money, I would need to keep this information to myself as I would always make time for her. There were some things that I felt that she didn't need to know about me. As for Steve and Nikki, I could get used to seeing them. After a while with them being around me so much, Steve would let up on asking me so many questions.

In front of me was the only chance that I might have being with someone that I did like to be around and maybe live out my life with. My mind was spinning and I didn't know what to do. The more I looked into her eyes and laid on that blanket with her, the more comfortable I became. She might be the woman that I have needed in my life for many years, and this opportunity might not come around but just this one time. So, I decided to tell her the story of me and Jenny, and see what her reaction was to what I told her. I needed to find out and give Taylor the chance to back away from me if she chose to.

"Thank you for sharing this with me. I am sure that it was hard for you to do," I said.

"It is something that I don't share with very many

people, Robert. I am making you an exception, though, as you have shown me a lot of kindness in the last couple of weeks since I arrived here. I have been with other men since the divorce, but when I was around them, they reminded me of Albert. All they wanted was what they could get from me, and they didn't really want to take the time to find out what I was all about first.

"You have wanted to know every time that we have been together if I was enjoying myself, and what makes me tick. You didn't need to take me around to see the sights that tourists come here to see. You chose to do this to make me happy, and give me something special to remember when I leave here without wanting something from me in return. This is why, Robert, I chose to tell you what I did today. I wanted you to know where I had just been, and the part of my life that I had that no one should have ever had to experience," Taylor responded.

"I can see that you had a rough marriage, and how you are afraid to get serious with anyone else as you might get hurt again, and how you don't want to be with the same kind of man that was like Albert, only to end up with the same life that you had with him. I would like to share with you my story, if you would like to hear it," I spoke.

"Yes Robert. I would. I have known that there was more to you than you have told me. Last night I stopped my uncle from asking too many questions because everyone has a skeleton in their closet that they don't want to talk about. I knew that if you didn't leave, he would keep asking you questions that might become personal ones that you don't want to share with any of us. When I told him that you might be tired and needed to leave, it wasn't meant to chase you away as I was trying to help you," Taylor commented.

"I appreciate what you did, Taylor. I like your uncle, and your aunt seems like a kind lady who really doesn't talk much. I have seen Steve a few times in the last 22 years of me living here. I know that he does like to talk. This is fine, but you are right as I, too, don't share much with anyone.

I have been damaged as well in a marriage that I was in 22 years ago. It also ended in a divorce. I, at times, wondered if I should feel regrets for the way that I ended the marriage and the choices that I chose for myself after I left. The reality is that I have no regrets on anything that I have done since then.

"I met my ex-wife, Jenny, one night while I was eating. She was a waitress. At the time she was new to her job and clumsy. She slipped on water that had been left on the floor behind me and fell. When she did, the tray that she was carrying with food and hot coffee ended up not just on me but her, too, as she fell to the floor. I was upset at first, but got up from my chair to pick her up. When we saw how each other looked, we both started laughing. This was the beginning of what I thought would be a lifetime of love together, not knowing that just months later, I would be anticipating the thoughts of how soon I could get away from her.

"We were both young and at that time I think it was more lust than love that led us down the aisle to get married. I had told Jenny from the very beginning of our relationship that I didn't want kids. She agreed that she would take precautions and that I wouldn't get any unwanted surprises. Well, this didn't last long as one night, after I had returned home from work, hungry and knowing that she would be waiting for me, so that we could eat dinner.

"Instead of this, Jenny told me that she had a huge surprise for me and that she wanted us to go out to eat to celebrate. I thought that maybe she had either found a new job that paid more money or that she had gotten a raise as a waitress, as you know waiting on tables doesn't get paid well. The tips she got were okay and did add to our income, which helped some when the bills came due, but at that time, being young and trying to get our careers to take off so that we wouldn't be as poor as we were, was a struggle for both of us.

"When we arrived at the place that Jenny had picked out for us to eat at, after I had sat down and we had ordered our food, Jenny blurted out that she was pregnant. At that moment I was shocked by her words. I stood up and said, *"You're* WHAT?" With me doing this, I had the attention of everyone in there until Jenny and I ate and left the place.

"After we had returned home, I confronted her with this, telling her that she had promised me that she would take precautions so that this didn't happen. She told me that she was, but that sometimes things happen. Then, of course, she started crying and told me that what she used must not have worked. At that moment, I knew that I couldn't stay with her anymore once she went into labor. I felt betrayed as I felt like I had been tricked by her, and that she knew what she was doing all along, and that she *wanted* to get pregnant. The reality was, she had stopped taking her birth control pills as I found the ones that she had in her purse and they were all there. The container indicated the date being months before that night. I knew she had lied to me.

"Many months went by, and as the baby grew inside her, the more excited she became. I found myself sneaking out at night to go to a club for female companionship. I was so hurt by Jenny that I didn't want to touch her ever again. Just months before her due date, Jenny got put on bed rest, which meant that she couldn't work any longer. This put more of a burden on me to work extra hours, to try to keep us afloat. I felt overwhelmed and knew that when it was time for her to deliver that I would be gone.

"Several weeks went by and I was still managing to get away at night, and also getting away with sleeping with other women. Then one day, I came home from work, and found Jenny waiting for me. A friend of mine had also been clubbing and saw me out cheating on Jenny, or should I say getting back at Jenny for lying to me. He went home and told his wife that he saw me, and what I was doing, and his wife told Jenny everything. At that moment, I really didn't care that she knew. Between all the crying and yelling that she did, it sent her into labor. She was bent over, telling me to take her to the hospital. She was in labor. I told her that I couldn't because I needed to go out of town on business with the company needing me to, and that we would need the extra money, especially now that the baby was being born. She begged me not to go, but I told her I had to. I called a taxi. I told the driver to take her to the hospital. Also, for him to take her inside and not to leave her until she was with a nurse or doctor. I paid him well for his time to do this.

"They left, and I finished packing my bags that I had started packing months before that day. After I had finished, I left the apartment and spent the night in a motel. The next day, when I was getting gas, a man that was in the hospital at the same time that Jenny delivered the baby came up to me. He couldn't wait to congratulate me on becoming a father of a baby boy. I didn't say a word back to him. I got in my car and left town, going East. I wanted to get as far away from Jenny and her baby as I could. I knew that her mother and father would take care of her and her son. Also, the state would help her, so I was on my own once again, and going to do whatever it took to make a good life for myself. Should I have regrets for my choice of what I did that night? NO! I felt nothing but betrayal and disgust for Jenny. This is how I ended up in Newark," I said to Taylor.

"Your story sounds much deeper than mine does. Maybe I should tell you that you did her wrong and everything that you did you should have done differently, but I do know that when a person loses trust in someone that they want to spend the rest of their life with and love, it becomes the most important thing to them. At that time, you felt hurt, betrayed and lied to," Taylor commented.

"Taylor, since then I have been with other women, but when I looked at them, I knew what they wanted. It wasn't anything that I thought I could deal with day after day for the rest of my life. The one-night stands became just that, and nothing more," I replied.

"We have covered a lot of ground today, from us walking in the park and Bushkill Falls. You know me better. I also know you better. This was something that was meant to happen. I won't judge you for what you did, Robert. You did what you thought that you needed to do in order to be happy within yourself. Since then, you have made a good life for yourself like I did when I chose to divorce Albert.

"Everyone's choices are their own, and whether they have regrets for what they choose is also their own. What you shared with me will stay between you and me. I am not sure that my aunt and uncle would have the same way of looking at this as we do. I am forever grateful for your honesty with me, and also your time that you have spent making sure that I am happy, and enjoying everything that we have done. For now, though, I need to return to the house My aunt wants me to go shopping with her tonight, and I shouldn't disappoint her. No, I am not making this up to get rid of you. I would like to see you again, whether we go anywhere special or just talk to each other. That would be good enough for me," Taylor remarked.

"I believe what you just said. Thank you for not mentioning this to anyone. I, too, have enjoyed our time together. We have laughed together and seen many tourist attractions that I hadn't seen since I have been here. Also, we have seen a different side of each other. I feel like we have become good friends, Taylor. I not only think that you are beautiful, but also a very classy lady. You have an elegant style about you, and don't ever change this. This morning I wasn't sure if we would see each other again after today because I have put up so many road blocks since trusting Jenny, and I didn't think that it would be possible for me to trust anyone again. I am not a perfect man. I do have other secrets that I keep to myself, but I feel that everyone does. I will take you home now, and will be calling you for another date," I replied.

"That would be very nice, Robert. Thank you," Taylor said with a smile.

That day, when I took her home, instead of just standing at the door, making sure that she got inside okay, I put my hand softly on her face and gently kissed her lips. I told her that I would be calling her very soon. I walked away.

My drive home was different than it had been. Before, I was convinced that I couldn't trust anyone with any part of my life. With Taylor telling me about a part of her life that she didn't need to share with me, I felt like I could share that small part of my life with her on how I ended up living in Newark. I felt like a lot of women, after hearing what I told Taylor, would have started screaming at me, telling me that I was a horrible person for leaving Jenny with a newborn son to raise by herself. Taylor didn't do this. It was like she heard my words and saw my heart. When I married Jenny, I had every intention in the world of staying with her the rest of my life. When she went behind my back to deliberately get pregnant without asking me first if I had changed my mind on not wanting kids, my trust in her was no longer there. From the time she broke the news to me, I became less interested in her. How could I stay with a woman that made me sick every time I looked at her?

Now that Taylor knew something about me, and I also knew something about her, we both would see if the attraction continued. I only had a week left to decide whether I was just infatuated with her because it had been quite a while since I had been with a woman, or if I was really ready to take a chance on another relationship, whether it be a long distance one or not. She might decide to quit her job in Chicago and move to Newark. If I started feeling trapped, or uncomfortable when I was around her, I would put the red flag in place.

I had gotten home and my work week was going to be a busy one every day. The inventory had increased, and more orders were scheduled to go on the trucks to ship out. With this going on, I would be making several trips around the company, to make sure that everyone was staying busy and working extra hard in order to fill all of the orders that we had.

Tomorrow morning I would be calling Taylor to invite her on a late-night dinner date. In my mind, half of my brain was telling me to take a chance again, and the other half was telling me to back away. The one thing that I did know was that if there turned out to be anything between Taylor and me, that I would *never* share what I did when I first came to Newark up until what I am doing now. There would be no reason for her to know as I would include her in the important parts of our relationship. This should be all that mattered as I wouldn't be another Albert to her.

In the morning, after grabbing a bagel and a cup of coffee to take with me to the office, I was out the door once again, trying hard to beat the traffic as I knew the best time to be on the freeways every day.

When I arrived at the company, I could see models walking up and down the halls. There was a fashion show scheduled for early afternoon. I was told to make sure that everything was in place and ready to go. No one but the rich were invited. With this, hopefully, sales would skyrocket.

I called Taylor and at that time only got her voicemail. I left her a message, telling her that I would like to see her tonight and that I would try calling her back later. This could be a bad sign after what she had heard yesterday, but I didn't think so. If she told her aunt and uncle what I said, they might have talked her out of seeing me again. I had too much to do today to assume something that I was sure hadn't happen. Whatever the reason why she didn't answer the phone was nothing that I could change.

That afternoon the fashion show was ready to go. The models were wearing expensive and elegant clothing when they walked down the runway. I looked at all the people that were there. All of them were wearing a smile. If this turned out good and sales increased even more, it would mean not just more money for this company, but also more money in my account.

Around 4:00 p.m., when I hadn't heard anything back from Taylor, I tried one more time to call her. This time she did answer her phone.

"Hello, Robert," Taylor said.

"Good afternoon, Taylor. It will be around 9:00 before I can pick you up tonight, if that works for you. I am buckled under with work this whole week and it is really going to be a busy one for me," I replied.

"That's fine. I am sorry that I missed your call earlier. My aunt took the day off today so that she could take me shopping. Last night after you left, Aunt Nikki and I did do some shopping. Today, we have been in just about every clothing store in Newark," she said as she chuckled.

"I am happy that you had fun today. I am pretty sure you will be having fun tonight as well. I will talk to you later, when I pick you up," I said.

"I can't wait, Robert. I'll meet you outside at your car at 9:00," Taylor spoke.

After we had our conversation, I sat at my desk and smiled. This was the first time that I had smiled from my heart in a long time.

At last the fashion show was over. Now it was time to see how many of the important guests that the company had invited would put in orders for the clothing that were modeled for them today. Hopefully as well, some of what wasn't worn by the models with this showing.

Before I knew it, the day of working was over for me. It was time for me to go back home and get ready for my date. The traffic was extra heavy on the freeways. I was hoping that I would be able to get to Steve's house and that I didn't end up stuck in a traffic jam going to get Taylor. Within an hour of getting ready, I was out the door and on my way to pick her up for a fantastic date night out.

Like other nights, Taylor was waiting for my car to pull up to the house and then she came out the door. This time I climbed out of my car and walked with her to the passenger side, holding her hand and opening the car door for her. She was dressed in an exquisite gown. Once again, what she was wearing looked like something that came from the company that I worked for. I told her she looked beautiful. She said thank you and smiled as we drove away.

Instead of just taking Taylor to a fancy restaurant tonight, I decided that we were really going to have some fun. We went to a nice club for not just a fabulous meal and drinks, but also for entertainment from only the best performers that were in the city at the time.

As we ate, we listened to Celine Dion perform many of her songs. Then Wayne Newton walked out on the stage. Celine took her bow and walked off stage. Everyone clapped for Wayne Newton and also listened to the songs that he sang. At the end of the performance, Celine and Wayne did a duet together and took bows at the same time! Taylor was so excited that she sat there and smiled big through the entire performance.

She told me that she had wanted to see them both in concert for years and could never get tickets to their shows. She said that tonight was very special as she got to watch them both in one night. She thanked me for bringing her there. It was getting late. I needed to take Taylor home as I had an early day tomorrow again. It would be a couple hours before I arrived at my home for sleep.

Tonight, when we pulled up in the driveway next to the house, Taylor laid her head on my shoulder and once again said, "Thank you so much, Robert. I had a great time tonight." Then she leaned toward my face and kissed me. At that time my heart melted and I felt like I hadn't felt for quite some time.

Taylor, I thought, was falling for me as well. I told her that I would pick her up again around the same time tomorrow night, and that I knew that she was going to have fun again. Taylor said that she was looking forward to it and that she would meet me at my car again. I then walked her to the front door where this time, I gave her a passionate kiss good night. She smiled and went inside.

My drive home once again was thinking of nothing but of how Taylor made me feel. I was even more excited for the next night of fun. I had a long day waiting for me again tomorrow at work. When I walked through my front door, I was ready for bed.

The next morning I was up early and ready to go to work, wearing a smile that wasn't fake this time. I was excited for that night with Taylor. She had a lot of fun at the club. Tonight would be much of the same thing with the exception of a different place to eat, with a different club and a different performer that was famous. If things worked out, tomorrow night I would take her to a different place other than a club as I didn't want to give her the impression that was what I did every night in my spare time. Whatever we did, or she picked to do, would be followed by a nice dinner at an elegant place to eat.

When I walked through my receptionist's door on my way to my office, my receptionist noticed that I looked happy and commented about it.

"Robert, you look very happy. I know that you smile a lot, but today there is a bigger smile on your face," Mary Beth remarked.

"Yes, I am very happy. There is a woman that I am interested in. We went out last night. Tonight we have another date. I am hoping that things work out between us," I said.

"If this girl makes you that happy, Robert, I hope that it works out good for you as well," Mary Beth said as she handed me the weekly inventory sales sheet.

When I looked at it, I couldn't believe my eyes. Our sales had tripled since last week. The fashion show was a huge success. This would mean not just more money in the company bank account, but also mine

I stayed busy the rest of the day. By the end of the day at work, I was ready to leave and get ready for yet another wonderful night with Taylor. When I did pick her up, we went to another elegant restaurant. After that, we went across the city to a different club, where she got to see Mariah Carey perform on stage. Later, she told me that she had been a fan for many years and that this made her night very special. Taylor was glowing, and couldn't stop talking about it and how much she had enjoyed the evening out together as we drove back to the house.

I had asked her where she wanted to go to the next night. Taylor told me that sometimes she just likes to see a good movie and sit in the theater, sharing a box of popcorn. She also mentioned that she would love to see my penthouse. I told her that we could do all of that, but that I would once again like to include a nice dinner before the movie. Taylor said that would be wonderful. Once again, she would meet me outside the house when I came to pick her up. I told her that I was sorry, but it would be another late night. She said that was fine. She would see me at 9:00. Once again, I placed my hand on her face gently and leaned into her to give her a passionate kiss good night as we stood at the front door.

My life looked like it was headed in a great direction. I couldn't be happier.

Work the next day went fast again. With me knowing that in three days Taylor was scheduled to leave to return home to Chicago, I was wanting to slow the clock down. I had some deep thinking to do. We both had some serious talking to do together. The next few days were going to be maybe the beginning of a new love for me, or the end of what might have been.

—6—

COMMITMENT

After I had been to the penthouse and made sure that it was presentable enough for Taylor, I was on my way to pick her up for a nice dinner somewhere and a movie that I had wanted to see called, *Chains*. I wasn't sure if Taylor would be into watching an action film, but I would ask her.

Like the last several days when I arrived, Taylor was ready to leave. She was dressed more casually tonight as I was, since our plans didn't involve wearing a suit and tie and an evening gown for her. We found a nice restaurant in the Bronx, and that was where we chose to eat.

The movie was also one that Taylor had said she had heard reviews on, and that she would be interested in seeing. So again I was scoring a 100. As we sat there watching the film and eating some popcorn, every so often she would lean her head over on my shoulder. When she did this, I would lean my head up against hers. When we were ready to leave there, Taylor once again told me that she was having a wonderful time and liked the movie very much.

Our next stop was at the penthouse. When we walked through the door, Taylor looked around and said, "Robert, I am impressed. Most bachelors don't keep their homes as nice as you do."

Then she chuckled and bent down to pick up one of

my dirty socks that I had been looking for. Then I started laughing as well. Once again, I could see the fun, playing side of Taylor.

"Thank you for taking me to all the places that you have in the last few weeks, Robert. It has meant a lot to me. You are so much fun to be around. It looks like we have a lot in common. I am very happy to call you my friend," she spoke.

"I too am very happy that you came into my life. I haven't made friends with anyone in the years that I have lived in Newark. I am not sure what is going on between you and me, Taylor. I know you make me smile for no reason, and even when I hear your voice on the phone, I feel comfortable around you, and as you can see from me spilling my guts to you about some of my life before now, I trust you. This is something that I haven't had in so many years.

"I can't wait to see you. When I kiss you, I feel something in my heart that I again haven't had for a long time. I know that in a few days you will be leaving here and going back home. I will miss you a lot. There is a part of me that wants to tell you to stay here with me, and then the other sensible side of me is saying that we need to get to know each other better.

"As you can see, my brain is all over the map. I am confused and not sure what the right way to feel is. Everything that I have told you didn't come from loneliness. I have been a loner for many years. It comes straight from my heart." I spoke, hoping that I hadn't just now shot myself in the mouth and ruined everything, or looked like a lovesick fool in her eyes.

"Robert, I understand everything that you just said. For me as well, it has been many years since I have been in a deep relationship with anyone. I, too, feel like we connect. We like the same food, the same entertainment, and I too have been a loner. I know many people like you do, but just consider them to be acquaintances. For years I, too, haven't been able to trust anyone, like you. This was all caused from being with Albert. The other night I felt very comfortable with you and also spilled my guts to you, wondering what you would think of me, and if you would ever want to see me again. I also get excited when the phone rings and I can see that it is you calling. I smile more now than I have in a long time.

"Even my aunt and uncle have commented on how I glow when I talk about you, or hear your voice on the phone. I do feel something when you hold me in your arms and kiss me. A part of me is doing the same thing that you are experiencing. I, too, am wondering if we are moving too fast, and wondering if we should slow down on the emotions that we are having. But as you know, sometimes it is easier said than done. I feel like we could be a match together after all of these years with both of us being alone.

"Yes, Robert, I do have feelings for you, but on Saturday morning I will be leaving here to go back to Chicago. This doesn't mean that we won't be talking to each other on the phone, and flying when we can, back and forth to see each other. I just feel like we should do the right thing and take it slow for a while. We need to get to know each other better as we both know that it won't always be the kind of life that we have had in the last three weeks with going out a lot and having fun. I feel like there is more to us than that, and this is the side that we both need to explore next before jumping into something that might go bad otherwise," Taylor responded.

"I know you are right, Taylor. If this does work out for us, I would want our love to last a lifetime just like you do," I said.

At that moment I kissed her and we hung onto one another for a while. I knew then that she was feeling the same way about me as I was her, and that we both would miss each other after she left. If we were meant to be, it would happen. She was right as by moving slowly, we would have the time to explore each other, to see if things continue to be the way that we felt right now, at this moment, before we made any kind of decision on what to do next.

Once again, I realized it is all about choices, and making the right ones.

For hours that night, Taylor and I sat on my couch, holding each other and at times kissing. We continued to talk and laugh. There was nothing sexual that happened and it felt good to both of us. She just needed to be loved in another way. I felt the same way. At about 2:00 a.m. I took her home.

That night I had so many thoughts going through my mind, causing me not to be able to sleep. All I could think about was Taylor and wanting her to stay there with me, so I could hold onto her, but I did understand what she was telling me when we talked. She had a level head on her shoulders and was looking for a full-time commitment, just like what I wanted after all of these years of trying to believe that I didn't need anyone anymore. She needed someone she could totally trust, just like I did, and someone that would respond not only to her words, but also to her needs.

I was sure that I could do this. We weren't kids any longer, and our last days on Earth needed to be complete and with someone that fulfilled not just our hearts, but our lives as well. I believed that Taylor was the woman that I had needed my entire life.

After she left, I was going to make sure that she knew that I would be with her as much as I could.

Right now, with all of the money in my account, I could quit my job and move close to her, but I felt like this wasn't what she wanted or needed at this time. She needed us to be apart to give both of us the chance to think about everything, to make sure that this was right for each of us.

Tomorrow I would be picking her up again to eat out, and no matter what was happening at work, I was going to Steve's home earlier than I had been, so that we could have as much time as possible to be with each other until she left on Saturday. I wasn't sure as of yet what we were going to do as Taylor and I didn't discuss this. We just said that we needed to spend time together. I would let her make the decisions on where we ate and where she wanted to go. I needed to show her that I would respect her feelings and what she wanted always, and that I would put her first in my life. My heart felt content and happy for the first time in many years. I laid in bed and smiled once again.

The next morning, when I walked through the door of my receptionist's office, she could see that my smile was not as big as it had been. There was no way for me to hide the feelings that I was having about Taylor leaving in a couple of days.

"Are you all right, Robert?" my receptionist asked.

"Yes, I am fine. I am just dealing with some emotions at the moment. I won't let them interfere with my work schedule today, though," I said with a fake smile.

"I know you won't," she said with a look on her face showing me that she really did care as I walked away from her desk to enter my own office. What was happening to me? If I wasn't careful, I was going to ruin the time left that Taylor and I did have together before she went back to Chicago. This was something that I didn't want to do.

I did my normal duties of the job requirement and it was early afternoon. The Robert before Taylor came into my life would have stayed at the office until 7:00 or 8:00 p.m., just to impress everyone and make it look like I was working harder than I was, but with this maybe being the last day and night with her, at around 1:00 p.m. I told my receptionist that I was leaving. I would see her in the morning. She had the reports that I had given her sitting on her desk, so would have plenty to do until she, too, left for the day.

Before I walked out the door of the building, I called Taylor and told her that I was going home to change, and that I would be there to pick her up in a few hours. Also, that today was going to be a casual day and that I was dressing accordingly. The place where I was taking her to eat was elegant, but not one where a man has to be wearing a suit and tie.

When we were on our way to the same restaurant that

we had eaten at before, I would talk to her about what she wanted to do and where she wanted to go.

At the restaurant we sat there, holding hands and smiling back and forth to one another. Taylor's eyes were beautiful, just like her smile. While we waited for our food, we talked more about future plans that included both of us. I was scheduled to fly to Chicago in a couple of weeks to see her. This time she would be the tour guide.

Taylor told me about a movie that she wanted to see called, *Bear Country*. We both agreed that we would drive to the Bronx again, where it was playing at the movie theater. As we sat and watched the action-packed film, we ate popcorn and held hands. Occasionally we would lean toward each other for a kiss. I could see that Taylor was having a good time as she told me that she had always wanted to visit Colorado. The movie was about a man that left the city to move to Colorado, where he bought a cabin in the mountains. Each day he encountered many things, from a near bear attack, to him walking around the lake not far from his cabin with many things happening to him. After the movie was over, once again Taylor thanked me for taking her to see it. She said she had a very good time.

Since it was still early in the day, she told me that she would like to go back to my penthouse, where we could do more talking. I was into that and wanted her to feel comfortable in my home as I was still hoping that someday it would be hers as well. As we sat there on the couch, holding each other, she told me about several things as I did her. None of these included Albert or Jenny in our conversation. She mentioned her growing up years, and for me, I too told her about my family, about my school, and what sport I was good at in high school. Once again, it wasn't a night of sexual activity. I wanted to respect Taylor, and I would know when she was ready for our relationship to go to the next level.

Around 2:00 a.m., we were standing at Steve's front door. This time it was extra hard for us to say good night as we would also be saying goodbye. Taylor told me that was the last night for us to be together as her Uncle Steve and Aunt Nikki wanted to spend the next day with her, and that she would be leaving very early Saturday morning to fly back to Chicago. She said that she couldn't wait until my visit in a couple of weeks.

Our bodies were close together and our arms were holding onto each other as if we weren't ever going to be together again. We continued to kiss each other, and neither one of us wanted to say good night, let alone goodbye. Finally, around 3:00 a.m., I told Taylor that I needed to leave and was looking forward to my trip in a couple of weeks. She said that even though she felt sad that she was also excited about me seeing Chicago, and especially her, because she felt like this was the start of a new chapter in our book of life and that we were about ready to write our story of a lifetime that we would have together. I held her face in my hand. For one last time I kissed her very gently on the lips. Then I walked away to return to my car and go back to my home to get ready for my day at work. There would be no sleep for me that night.

The only thing I knew to do when I returned to my home was to drink lots of coffee as I was going to need the caffeine that day in order to make it through work. I sat on the couch, thinking about what many people would say if they knew the story of my life since I left Jenny. I was sure that they would tell Taylor to run for the hills, and ask me how a con artist can love anyone but himself, and think that I was just pulling another con with this one being on Taylor. No matter what, I wanted to share my life with her, but I could *never* tell her my story of what I really did for a living all these years. If I did, it would be the end of us for good.

Once again at work. I sat at my desk, thinking about all of the conversations that we'd had, and imagining us together living in my penthouse and being able to hold each other each day. I had fallen head over heels in love with Taylor. I didn't want to let her go *ever*. I wanted to call her on the phone and tell her not to leave Newark, and that she could stay with me, and that I would always take care of her. I wasn't sure if it was too soon for that conversation, and didn't want to come across to her as being pushy. She had said that she wanted us to get to know each other better and that we both could do this through trips of either me going there to see her or her coming back here to see me.

A few times I picked up the phone to call her, to try to talk her into staying. Then I closed my phone and sat it down on my desk. I was going to let her call me. It wasn't long after thinking this when my phone did ring. It was Taylor calling.

"Hello, Robert. How is your day going so far?" she asked.

"I am okay. I am missing you, but trying to stay as busy as I can. Have your plans for the day changed?" I asked.

"No, they are still the same. I just wanted to call you because I also miss you and wanted to hear your voice again. I know that this is going to be hard for both of us being apart for now, but I feel that we are doing the right thing, and it is for the best. I want you to get to know all about me as I do you before we make a decision on where we take our relationship to next. I hope that you still feel the same way," Taylor replied.

"I understand, and if this is what you choose and want, then this is what I choose to do as well. I hope that you have a good day with your aunt and uncle as they have been very understanding, sharing you with me while you have been here. I will give you a call later this evening and we can talk for a while before we both need to go to sleep. I know that you have an early flight out in the morning, so I won't keep you on the phone forever. I miss you, Taylor, and you haven't even left yet," I said.

"I miss you too, and will talk to you later," she spoke.

After hanging up the phone, I sat it down on my desk and my smile had turned upside down. I had really wanted to ask her not to leave, but it sounded like she had her mind made up, and I wasn't sure if I could change it right now. This was the choice that she made, and I guess me as well.

That night after returning back home, I called Taylor for

the last time today. She was happy that I had called her. We stayed on the phone, talking for a couple of hours. She told me that her aunt and uncle were happy that she had stayed to visit with them today. We talked a little while longer, and then she announced that she had to go to sleep. We not only said our good nights, but also said our goodbyes. I laid in bed, once again thinking until I fell asleep.

The next day I tried calling Taylor. Her phone went to voicemail, which told me that she was on the plane. I leaned over in bed and looked at the clock. I was right.

I wanted to cry, but held back tears. I was wondering how a woman could be changing a con artist's way of thinking, and how I was allowing it to happen. For many years I had a cold heart that wouldn't let anyone in, and now my thoughts were returning to many years ago when I had allowed Jenny into my life. Maybe this was because I was older now, and knew that there would come a day when I would want a woman to be with me until the end, and when I took my last breath.

When I looked in the mirror that day, I saw a different side of me. It was a side that I thought would be dead and buried for the rest of my life. It was time for me to regroup and make sure that being in a long-distance relationship was what I wanted.

I went to work that morning, feeling a little run over, but before the day at work had ended, I did receive a call from Taylor, letting me know that she had arrived in Chicago safely and was missing me as much as I was missing her. Once again, she told me that she was looking forward to my visit in a couple of weeks, and to call her later on tonight. That night I did call her and the next couple of weeks seemed to fly by.

Soon I was headed to Chicago and very happy again. Taylor was there at the airport, waiting for me. We stood at the gate my plane arrived at, holding each other in our arms for quite a while before we left and went to her house.

Taylor was the tour guide like I had been while I was

there, and one of the places that we visited was the Chicago Bears football stadium. She also took me to see where she worked.

My time off from work went by very fast, and I was sitting back in Newark at my desk, waiting for the next visit. This would be with Taylor coming here again to see me, and staying this time at my penthouse.

Our trips back and forth to see each other became more frequent, and within six months we were in a solid relationship. It was Taylor who was once again coming to see me as I had a board meeting that I wasn't going to miss.

The company had tripled their profits and I had also benefited as well. I was starting to see big amounts of money coming into my bank account each week. I knew that I could give Taylor the kind of lifestyle that she should have. I had bought her a beautiful engagement ring that I was going to put on her finger if the answer was yes when I took the big step. I was going to ask her to be my wife.

As I sat in the airport, I took the ring from my suit pocket, and looked at it. The diamond in the ring was large in size and very classy.

There were 30 minutes left before the plane was scheduled to arrive. I was smiling and happy and content, sitting there waiting on her. At that moment, I heard over a loud speaker that Flight 10, for American Airlines scheduled to arrive, had crashed and that fire trucks were at the scene, watering the plane, in hopes of finding live passengers.

I completely lost it! I stood up and yelled as loud as I could, "NOOOOO!" My heart was broken and I was so afraid. If I was right, I had lost Taylor forever! I took her engagement ring from my suit pocket and threw it on a seat that I was sitting on!! I checked my phone to make sure there wasn't a missed call from Taylor, telling me that she had changed her mind in coming to Newark, and instead would wait for me to return to Chicago. There was no missed call.

I went to the ticket agent and asked a woman if she could look to see if Taylor was on the plane. When I was told that yes, Taylor was on that flight, my heart felt like it had snapped in two! I felt so much pain and so much guilt, and many regrets! I was the one who was supposed to be on that plane and not Taylor. It was my choice for her to come here again because of a stupid meeting that I could have gotten out of. The regret that I was feeling inside was more than I thought that I could ever have, as I had always felt like I had and would NEVER feel regrets again.

At that time, the ticket agent picked up the phone and told me to stick around for a few minutes. After she was completely done talking, she looked at me with sadness in her eyes and told me that she had just gotten news that all of the passengers riding that plane were declared dead. The crash was a bad one with no survivors. I stood and cried like I hadn't ever cried before! I felt betrayed again in a different way.

I knew that I had to call Steve and Nikki and let them know what happened. With tears running down my face, it was hard to see the numbers on my phone to dial their number. When Steve answered, he was excited to hear from me and asked me if maybe with this visit Taylor and I could stop by the house for a short visit one of the nights while she was back here. I started crying even more, and then I had to tell him that he would never see Taylor again as the plane that she was on had crashed with no one found alive on it.

Out of feeling devastated, he started screaming and crying too. He lashed out at me and said, "If it wasn't for you, Robert, Taylor would still be alive!! *You* should have been the one that died!"

With hearing this, I hung up my phone and left the airport. I knew he was right and my tears kept flowing until there were none in there to come out! By then I was bitter and didn't care whom I hurt in the process. I had lost it, *and* my mind!

From that moment on, I continued to con everyone that I knew and could hurt in the process. My life had taken a spiral and I didn't care. I made a lot more money from

Heatherton Incorporated, and even more money any other way where I could.

I felt that the reason why I had lost Taylor was because of karma from all the bad things that I had done and continued to do, and in my mind it wasn't fair. My sick excuse that was giving me permission to do this was because I felt justified taking from the rich people because they seemed to be the only ones that had a good stable life without heartache and pain. The truth was that the rich people also had problems and experienced pain just as much as I had.

I was the one who had the biggest problem all those years and it was called greed! My life as I saw it becoming, with having Taylor for my wife, would never be the same way again. I would never find another woman like her, so I was just going to live out my life without a commitment of any kind from another woman. Although that didn't stop me from being the player that I had been before and going to clubs every night to pick up a woman and take her to a sleazy motel room for the night.

After working for Heatherton Incorporated for five years, it was time to take my money and run. I gave my resignation to Mr. Heatherton. Of course he said he hated to see me go. If he only knew what I had done to him, and all the more money that he would have in the company bank account, he wouldn't have hesitated to hurt me or make sure I paid for what I had done, living out a big part of my life in jail.

I was done with Newark and each day driving in that city made me sick. I headed west in the direction that I had come from 27 years ago, leaving Newark with no return ticket for me. I sold my penthouse and was going back in the direction of where my roots began. By then I had spent the biggest part of my living in a city and was ready to return to small towns once again.

As for Steve and Nikki, I never saw them again. I knew that they would continue to blame me for the death of Taylor, and they were probably right as I continued to blame myself. I knew that I could have missed that meeting and gone to

Chicago as planned, but instead I chose to stay because of money and wanting to know just how much more was going to be put in my bank account.

Because of this and the way that Taylor loved me, she had agreed to come to Newark to please me. This whole thing was my fault, like Steve had said. But even though I knew this, my bitterness inside my body took over my mind. My thoughts back then were that the only one that I cared about or would ever care about again was myself for the rest of my life.

—7—

SHOULD I STAY, OR LEAVE?

After remembering this from years ago, it was time for me to return to the present instead of living on the past choices and regrets that I had made that might affect me the rest of my life. Did I miss Taylor? Yes, very much so! I believe that she would have been the woman that changed my life forever. For every action there is a reaction, and because of what I chose, the reaction was something that I had to live with forever.

I was sure that the coin was staying with me for a reason. I am sure that even if I didn't pick it up that day off of Jenny's grave, it would have somehow magically appeared to me. Whatever the reasoning was behind it, I hoped that it became known to me soon!

I looked around the room, and it looked to me like the diner was ready to close for the night. The help was putting chairs on top of the tables, and before long someone would be coming to me, asking me to leave.

I had sat there long enough, and I needed to go back to the motel room to see if Kelly had called me back.

Being a much older man than I was many years ago, I think about things that I wouldn't have even thought about before. It was like Jenny talking to me from her grave. Could I have just imagined this happening or did it really happen?

I hadn't worked in a couple of years and was living off of what most people would call stolen money. I wasn't the richest man in the world, but I had enough in the bank for many lifetimes with *no* regrets of what I had done from the choices that I had made to get it. I would live out the rest of my life alone because I knew that I couldn't buy happiness at any cost.

Once again, I returned to the motel room with no flashing light on the motel answering machine. I was convinced that Kelly was not going to call me back. I had a decision to make and that was whether I still wanted to live out my life in this small town, or move on down the road. Something kept telling me in my head that I needed to stay.

Since the first day here, everything had been weird. The blast from the past had come back to haunt me in different ways. I had been thinking a lot about my younger years ,which I wasn't doing before I had seen David at Jenny's grave site for the first time, and the flashing coin continued to stay with me no matter where I went, or where I put it before I left the motel. It always ended up in my pocket. I was sure that if I took the coin back out to Jenny's grave that it would once again appear wherever I was.

It had been another long day for me. I wasn't getting proper rest. I did what I had done every night at the motel. I sat and drank coffee for hours before I even tried to go to bed, wondering what was next. I should not feel as unsettled as I am.

I had an appointment with the Realtor in the early part of the afternoon the next day, and by then I needed to make sure that this was for certain where I wanted to be. I had been driving from town to town for many years, and not knowing where I belonged next. Maybe Apple Grove would give me the peace that I was looking for. Some people would say that with everything I had done to others, I didn't deserve peace or a good life. The night that I lost Taylor in the airplane crash, I still feel like at that moment my life ended as well.

After drinking a pot of coffee while sitting on the couch, thinking about many things, I fell asleep. I had given up on hearing from Kelly, so when I did leave the motel room, I would forget about her calling me back.

In the morning, I had only a few hours of sleep. I had to make a decision on whether to stay or leave for good. Apple Grove was a nice, small town, unlike Newark. Most of the time it was quiet and peaceful.

As I was getting ready to walk out the door, the motel phone finally rang.

"Hello." I said.

"Robert, it is Kelly. Why did you call me?" she asked.

"I heard about Jenny, and so I came here to Apple Grove to visit her grave. I was wondering if we could get together to talk," I replied.

"I'm not sure, Robert. When you left, it was a struggle for Jenny and David, your son. I have been upset with you for many years now and I am not sure that there is anything for us to talk about," Kelly spoke.

"I know that you have only heard one side of the story about why I left, and I would like to tell you my side. Also, I would like for you to tell me about how Jenny passed away. Is there a way that you will meet me just one last time so that we can talk?" I asked.

"I guess, Robert. I wish I could say that it would be a pleasure to see you again, but I can't," Kelly responded.

"I understand, and I promise you that this will be the last time that I ask you to meet me anywhere. Can you come to the diner tonight at 7:00?" I asked.

"I should be able to. I am meeting a client at 2:00 this afternoon, and should be there around 7:00 tonight. If you want me to tell you that what you did to Jenny and David was all right, you called the wrong woman," Kelly replied.

"No, Kelly, I don't expect this from you or anyone else. I will see you at 7:00 p.m. at the diner," I said as I hung up the phone.

From the sound of Kelly's voice, she still had hard

feelings toward me and being Jenny's best friend, I could see why. If she thought that I would apologize to her for what I did, she was in for a letdown as I have no regrets for what I did that day.

I was going to go ahead and buy that house. If I didn't like it here, I would just sell it and move on. That was my plan. I signed what papers the Realtor had given to me. I gave her a check for the house, and it was mine. I was told that since everything had been taken care of, I could move in any time that I chose to.

The house was in the best neighborhood, and was the nicest and largest house in the area. It had a long circle driveway, just like the one that Steve and Nikki had in Newark. Only the best for me. I was ready to get out of that motel. Maybe now, after I had moved into the house, my life would get back to normal and my dreams and thoughts would change. Time would tell.

In the morning I would check out of that motel. I went shopping for furniture and also other items that I was going to need.

I arrived at the diner to wait for Kelly. At 6:50 p.m., she walked through the door. She was as beautiful as ever and didn't look like she had aged a bit. She saw me and walked over to the table.

"Hello, Kelly," I said.

"Hello, Robert. I am not sure why you wanted to see me again, but I decided to come here anyway," Kelly responded.

"Kelly, I know that you are mad at me for what I did to Jenny and David. I would like the opportunity to tell my side of the story. If you don't understand after that, then I will accept it. Also, I would like to know what happened with Jenny and David after I left. I went to visit Jenny's grave and also would like to know what she died from," I spoke.

"Robert, when Jenny found out that you had left town instead of coming to the hospital to be with her and see your newborn son, it broke her heart. She had a hard time giving birth to your son and needed you by her side. Instead, you up and ran away, leaving her there in a strange place and not being there when she needed you to hold her hand and wipe away the sweat from her forehead while she gave birth," Kelly replied.

"Kelly, I have my reasons for leaving when I did. If you will listen to me, you will know exactly why I left her and David."

"I will listen, Robert, but that doesn't mean that I will agree with what you did," Kelly commented.

"That's all I am asking of you, Kelly. I just want you to hear the whole truth to the story," I said.

At that time the waitress had come to our table and was ready to take our order. We told her what we wanted and she walked away. Then we resumed the conversation.

"Months went by after we had married, and we were struggling financially. Neither one of us at the time would accept help from our family. Jenny wasn't making much money working as a waitress, and her tips were okay, but not a huge amount. Being a construction worker at the time, my job was seasonal, and during the winter months because of the bad weather, I wasn't able to work and had to work doing odd jobs or any other kind of job that I could get that didn't pay much. We were poor and were barely keeping our head above water and didn't need an extra mouth to feed.

"The night that she told me that she was going to have a baby, I had come home tired from work, expecting to see the same pot of pinto beans warming on the stove that we would have for dinner. Instead, I was told that she had something important to tell me and that we were going out to eat to celebrate the good news. At that time, I said okay as I thought that maybe she had found a better paying job or even gotten a raise at work. We couldn't afford to do this, but I agreed that we could go.

"After we had ordered our meal at the restaurant, Jenny told me that she was going to have a baby. This was something that I didn't expect, especially after Jenny's speech before we got married, telling me that I didn't *ever* need to worry about this happening.

"I stood up in the restaurant and said something that drew attention to us until we left the place. We didn't talk on the way home to ... as you remember ... the small apartment built for two people that we could barely afford. When we did get back there, Jenny could see that I was not happy and I reminded her about how she had promised me that we would have no children. Of course she cried, and said that sometimes things happen. She said that she had been taking precautions and that it didn't work. Yes, sometimes this does happen, but with me counting on her to make sure that she took something to keep her from getting pregnant, I didn't use anything for precaution.

"She had lied to me because while she was in the bedroom getting ready for bed and crying, I saw her purse sitting on the chair. I knew that she always kept her birth control pills in it, and that she always took one in the morning before she went to work. I did find the birth control pills, but the date on them was dated the month that I met her. She had been lying to me all that time of our marriage and before then. I had the proof of it in my hands.

"As she got bigger and the baby was growing, she was very happy and expected me to be. She wanted the child and I wasn't going to deny her from having the baby. The only thing that I knew to do was to leave her before she had the baby, so I started packing small things and hiding the bags in the closet. This way, Jenny wouldn't know what I was about to do. If she did know, she would have gone into early labor and her baby wouldn't have been born.

"Of course, my family, hers, and even you, Kelly, were very happy when you heard the news. I remember you telling me, 'Robert, now that you are going to be a father, don't screw it up.' At the time, I remember smiling at you, but in my mind it was a smile meaning that I wouldn't be around here much longer to screw anything up.

"Then, a few months later, as you know, she almost lost the baby and quit her job. This put extra weight on my shoulders as I was the only one working and at that time, I was thankful that it was in the summer as I could go back to my old job such as it was. Even with this, though, I worked for a small company in a small town and the pay was okay, but not the best, so I had to work extra hours in order to buy food and pay bills. We were struggling even more. I couldn't wait to get out of there. Over the months to follow, our sex life was gone as I didn't trust her and knew that I never could again. All I felt for her because she had lied to me was disgust and that wasn't changing.

"The night that I left her for good, one of my friends had seen me many times at different clubs with other women. He had gone home and told his wife about it, and she chose to tell Jenny what I was doing at night when she was asleep. I came home from work and Jenny started yelling at me and we were arguing about everything. She bent over in pain and told me that she was in labor and to take her to the hospital. I told her that I couldn't as I had to go out of town on business and we needed the extra money after she gave birth.

"She told me not to go, but I told her that I was, and then I called a taxi for her. I told the driver to take her to the hospital and not to leave her alone until she was with a doctor or a nurse. I paid him well to do this with the money that I had been saving back each month for my exit out of town, so that I would be as far away from Jenny as I could get.

"That night I had taken everything that I wanted and left the house. I knew that her parents and my family would help her and that she could draw money from the state as well. So, I had no regrets at what I was about to do. That night I stayed in a motel, and the next morning went to see an attorney to fill out paperwork for a divorce and for the papers to be served after I had left town.

"That morning a man that I knew happened to be at the hospital the night before and had heard that Jenny had given birth to a baby boy. He congratulated me on being the father of a son. All I did was look at him, get in my car, and leave, going East, where I have been until a few years ago.

"I guess why I wanted you to know the whole story, Kelly, is because there are always two sides to any story, and with you being Jenny's best friend, I was sure that she would leave out important parts, like the part about lying to me about taking her birth control pills. If she was lying to me about that, she was lying to me about other things, and I couldn't stand being around her," I said, expecting Kelly to get up from her chair and storm out of there in a huff.

"Robert, I don't know what to say or, to be honest, what parts of your story to believe. I do know, though, that Jenny should have told you about the birth control pills still sitting in the container for months of not taking them. She didn't tell me about this. I knew that you were having problems, and when I asked if there was any way that I could help, she told me no and that you both would work things out. I had no idea that you were struggling so hard financially at that time. I don't approve of the way that you left her that night. She did deserve to have you there with her at the hospital in the delivery room. Because you weren't there, I got a call from a nurse, asking if I would come to the hospital to be there for support for her in the delivery room, and as for David, he was innocent in this whole thing and didn't ask to be born.

"Jenny didn't remarry after you left her. She had a bad trust issue and because she was beautiful, there were men that did ask her out on a date. When they wanted a kiss good night, she would turn her head and tell them that she needed to go inside to take care of her baby. Many times I would try to talk to her, to reassure her that you leaving her was not the end of the world, and that there was life after you, but it was the same reply every time. She said, 'I'm not interested anymore.'

"David grew up with Jenny and her mother, as Jenny's father passed away around a year after you left. When he died, once again it was a heartache that Jenny had to endure and she told me that everyone that she loved had left her. Her mind was depressed and she couldn't pull herself out of the depression. She didn't show this side to David, though, as she wanted him to grow up good and normal. He did. After high school, he joined the military and spent three years overseas. He fought alongside the other soldiers and became a man. Jenny didn't know what to do with herself when David was gone. He had become her world and the only man that she ever trusted. After David got out of the military, he took out a loan and bought a construction company. Heavy equipment always fascinated him, and during his military tour this was what he did. It was his job, so he was familiar with every piece of equipment that was made.

"Jenny was a great mom to David, and he did very well in school. When David was born, she went back to her job being a waitress. She did this for a few years and then felt bad because she was taking money from her mother's retirement fund that her mother and her father had saved for years. From there, she went to a community college in town and took classes at night so that she could support her and David without help. When she graduated from the college, she had a business degree and so she got a job as a legal secretary with a lady attorney in town. She was very good at this job and did make a bunch more money than she did being a waitress. So, their life wasn't bad after that. Jenny took care of her mother as well until her mother passed away. This sent Jenny into another depression, where she ended up in the hospital for a week.

"She was lonely, but too stubborn to take a chance at life again. There were many times when she would bring up your name to me. She said that she hated you for what you had done to her and David. Of course, once again, I didn't know the missing parts that you told me, and if I did, I might have been able to help her even more than I did.

"As for your own family, I haven't seen any of them for many years. I have no idea even if any of them are still alive. I would hope that you kept in contact with them over the years, and had talked to them about the same thing that you just told me.

"Jenny suffered from a rare blood disease, Robert. The doctors gave her many blood transfusions, trying to straighten her blood out, and nothing worked. She spent a lot of time in the hospital and finally had to give up her job as she only got worse. David thought that the best place for her was in a nursing facility as he couldn't be with her 24 hours a day, and his wife couldn't either as he had married by then, and was also a dad. David would take his family to visit Jenny as often as he could, and toward the end of her life she had gotten so bad that she didn't even recognize any of them. They had also discovered that she had a form of Dementia and there was nothing that they could do about this either. You have missed out on a lot since you have been gone, Robert," Kelly replied.

"No, Kelly, I haven't talked to or seen any of my family since the last time that they came over to the apartment to congratulate Jenny and I on being parents before long. I knew that they were furious with me, and that if I did try to tell my story of what really happened, they probably wouldn't believe anything that I said. Since I left Jenny, I have made a good life for myself. I have seen a lot of the world and had really good jobs which paid very well. I am sure that you are mad knowing this, because of the way that Jenny lived, but everyone has choices and it is up to them to decide whether they want to take their life in a certain direction.

"I am sorry that Jenny had to struggle for what she had until she got her degree and became a legal secretary. I am sure she was very good at her job. I know that David helped her as much as he could. I am happy that he found a good life for himself. I hope that when Jenny passed away that she wasn't in pain. I don't wish that on anyone. You might think that I am self-centered and arrogant. I, too, worked very hard to get what I have now. Some of what I did wasn't easy and for many years I couldn't find myself trusting another woman. They were fine for a one-night stand, but not the kind of women that I wanted to spend my life with.

"The only woman that came close to being my match was named Taylor. She was perfect in my eyes, and one night when she was flying in to the airport, the plane crashed and everyone on board was killed. I was told later that the landing gear was iced up, and so when the plane hit the runway, it skidded off of it and crashed with the plane bursting into flames. This only made me more bitter than I was before, and since then I have continued to use women the way that I wanted to. So, you might say that I have been a player looking for a good time and a one-night stand.

"I saw David the other day at the cemetery. I was standing next to Jenny's grave when I saw his car come flying down the cemetery road. At the time, not knowing that he was my son, the only thing I was thinking about was that some punk was driving too fast in there.

"When I went back to Kingston, where Jenny and I lived, a neighbor of ours came over to me and had recognized me. He said that he was sorry to hear about Jenny. I told him that Jenny and I were not together and hadn't been for many years. He, of course, told me that he was sorry and that Jenny had died. I asked him where she was buried and he told me that Jenny wanted to be buried in her hometown of Apple Grove. That is why I came here. I felt that I should pay my respects to her grave site.

"The man that knew me had a son that was friends with David. He told his son that he had seen me and what kind of car I drove and also what I looked like. David, being a smart man, watched for me. When I arrived here, he saw my car and followed me up to the cemetery. There he proceeded to tell me what a piece of crap dad that I was and how he would never leave a wife that was pregnant and do to her what I had done to Jenny. He told me his name was David and he was my son. Then he walked away and, of course, peeled out with his car, once again driving way too fast to get away from me. I had told him that I had no regrets for what I had done then and the rest of my life. If I had told him the story that I told you just now, with him being so mad at me, he wouldn't have believed me anyway. The other night I saw him in here, sitting and eating with a woman and a child. I wondered if that woman was his wife and if the child is his. Now I know that they are a happy family. I am glad that he has a good life and a woman that he can trust. Did Jenny get to spend any time with the child before she passed away?" I asked.

"Yes, Robert, she did. I, too, was in a relationship that went sour. The only difference was that we were together for many years before I left him. I also had a trust issue unlike the one that you had with Jenny, but one that also devastated me when it ended. I made the choice to end our marriage and it was the best thing for me. Now that we have eaten and talked, I need to drive back to my home. With the story that you told me, I can't honestly say that I believe everything that you told me, but some of what you said makes sense to me because of conversations that Jenny and I had. Take care, Robert, and I hope that you can find some inner peace within yourself," Kelly said as she got up from her chair and walked away toward the door.

If Kelly only knew what all I did after I left Jenny, she would think that me leaving Jenny was a minor thing compared to all of the people that I had hurt over the years. Did I have any regrets with any of it? *No,* I didn't!!

As I walked out of the diner, I was going back to the motel, hopefully for the last time. I wasn't sure what Kelly was thinking about on her way home, but regardless of her thoughts, at least she had heard the truth from me. This was a subject that I wouldn't bring up to David as I knew that he wouldn't believe a word that I said anyway. There was no way, even if he did believe me, that I would tell him the truth as he truly loved his mother and I was sure that he was still having some emotional issues because of her death.

Even though things didn't go right with Jenny and me, she had been a good mother to him, and if I couldn't respect her for anything else, at least I could respect her for that. He was raised good and much better than he would have been if I had stayed with Jenny, feeling sorry for her. I knew for years before I had even met her that I couldn't be a good father, and it wouldn't have mattered how many years we were together, I wouldn't have changed my mind on wanting to be one. Being forced into it was not what I ever wanted and this was what basically Jenny did to me.

As for Kelly, she could believe whatever she wanted to. I have no regrets for what I did and there was a part of me that felt like when she was talking, she was trying to make me feel guilty for my choices that I had made. It didn't work.

As I walked through the door to my motel room, I was exhausted. There would be no sitting up drinking coffee for me that night as I needed some sleep.

Like every night since I had been in Apple Grove, I reached into the pocket of my pants to empty them to put the things I had in there on the dresser. Once again, the flashing coin was in there, trying to tell me something, but WHAT???

That night I was so tired that within five minutes I was sound asleep. It was around 9:00 a.m. when I woke up the next morning. After drinking some coffee and getting ready, I was out the door to pick up some more items for my new home, and shortly I would be going straight to the house so that I would be there when the furniture truck pulled up in the driveway. This day was hopefully the start of a new life for me in Apple Grove.

By the end of that day, I had everything I needed moved into my new home, which was a beautiful mansion. Not bad for a man that spent years being poor until he learned that in order to help himself, he had to help himself to another person's money.

The only item missing in my new home was a land line phone, which I chose not to have. A con man never keeps the same number for very long. All of the cell phones that I had in the past had been stepped on and broken before I threw them in a large trash dumpster.

That night I sat on my couch, thinking once again about what had taken place after I left Newark. I had decided that I needed some entertainment once again. My destination at that time was Las Vegas. Being older, I wasn't quite as cocky as I was in my younger years. I still had an ego like I do now, and at that time because of the death of Taylor and the bitterness that I was feeling inside, I didn't care what woman I hurt as I thought of myself as a lady's man.

I had visited Vegas one other time before I met Jenny, when I had turned 21 and still lived in Kingston. This time being a much older man and the second time of being there, the morning that I arrived in Vegas, I was driving down the strip, admiring all of the beautiful hotels. I had decided to stay at the Mirage Hotel and Casino.

When I pulled up in front of it, a valet came over and asked if I was staying there and I told him yes. He then took my car to park it in the hotel parking lot after I grabbed my suitcase from my car.

I went to the reservations desk and paid them for a few nights of staying in their luxury hotel. There was a lot that I wanted to see while I was there, but my first stop would be checking out my room, showering, changing clothes and trying my luck at the roulette table. Then, if I still felt like winning more money, I would play blackjack and see what happened at that table. When I was young, and had gone there before I met Jenny, I spent a bunch of time with an older man who taught me a lot about roulette and blackjack. He was winning thousands of dollars, and he told me that there was a trick to it and that if I hung out with him, he would teach me what he knew. For many days I did hang out with him, and by the time I left Vegas, I knew every trick in the book, and where to put my chips, no matter what the odds were against me.

I had finished in my room and took the elevator down to the casino. My first stop in there was the roulette table. I didn't waste my time on the slots as the chances of winning on them are like one in a thousand, if not more than that.

The odds of winning anything is always better at the tables. I found one and sat down to play some roulette. With a pocket load of money and all the time in the world at that moment, I had a feeling that I was going to walk away with more money than what I had laid down when I was buying the chips.

After I sat down in the chair, a tall thin guy with a big cigar sticking out of his mouth kept looking at me. He, too, was sitting at the big table across from me and sitting next to many people who also felt lucky. He was staring me down and I felt like he was daring me to buy a bunch of chips and lose every dime that I had the first spin of the wheel.

I watched the ball spin to see where it landed. It showed one of my numbers as I was playing even money, and working with the same strategy that had been taught to me many years ago. Finally, after the man kept watching me, I decided that I would strike up a conversation with him and see what he had on his mind.

"Do you come here much?" I asked.

"Yes, I am a regular at this table. Be prepared to lose all of your money tonight as I am good at this game," the man said.

How little did he know that he might be good, but I happened to be better, so I answered him.

"I'm also pretty good at roulette, so I guess we will see who walks away with the money," I replied.

The man gave me a dirty look and still kept watching where I put my chips. He seemed to think that the numbers that he chose were better, and with him doing this, he kept losing more money. The wheel kept spinning and once again the ball landed on one of my numbers. At that time, we were playing for some big bucks and the man was getting more and more irritated. In his mind he thought that he was the best and didn't like it because I was there and the one winning. At one point he even thought that each game was being rigged and accused me of working for the casino and cheating. I had to laugh at him, which didn't go well as he stood up with his cigar in his mouth and a drink of some sort in his hand, and left the table. From there, he went to the blackjack table, where he once again bought a bunch of chips to play the game 21, in hopes that his cards were better than the dealer's hand.

I stayed where I was for about an hour, and then after raking in more money than I had spent, I decided to also try my luck at blackjack. I decided not to sit at the same table as that guy did as he still kept staring at me, and when I was winning, and he wasn't, he once again got very angry and this time he decided to threaten me.

"I will see you later! Not in here, but outside in a street somewhere! You think you are pretty smart! Let's see how good you are with your hands as I am going to make sure you are hurting really bad!"

At that time the dealer had pushed a button that was under his table and the security guards showed up to haul him out of here. He was drunk and disorderly and wanted to knock my head off. With everything that I had done to innocent people, I was sure that he wasn't the only one who wanted to do this.

I stayed at the table for about an hour with me once again winning. Blackjack was my game and I was good at it as well. My cards were higher than the dealer's cards, and I kept winning every hand. When I had all of the cards that I wanted, I waved my hand over them. The dealer then knew that I didn't want anymore. It was time to walk away.

When I got up from the table, I noticed a couple of men in suits that kept looking at me. No matter where I went in the casino, they were not far away. I wasn't sure if they were this guy's bodyguards and had come to make good on his promise, or if they were detectives thinking that I had pulled off a scam at the tables as I had taken the casino for quite a bit of money.

After walking around for a while and sticking some coins in a slot, I was watching to see if the two men were still close by. They were, but I knew that if they were detectives for the casino, as long as I wasn't doing anything wrong there would be no way that they would arrest me. It would be hard for them to make anything stick in court if they thought that I was cheating at the roulette table and doing something shifty as well at the blackjack table, so once again I was convinced that more than likely it had to be a couple of thugs that were hooked up with the man sitting there threatening me. Maybe they were waiting for me to leave the casino, so that they could make good on the threat and beat me up in an alley somewhere.

I wasn't planning on staying in there forever, so I had to make it look like I wasn't watching them as well. I walked away from the casino and went to a buffet in the hotel lobby. As long as I stayed around people, I felt like the two men wouldn't try anything with me. I sat there for another hour, eating and watching people come and go, hoping that these men would get tired and leave. Unfortunately, they didn't and stayed close by to where I was.

It was time to leave the cafeteria and this time I walked out the door of the casino with a bunch of people that were in a group and stayed close to them. For all the thugs might have thought I came to Vegas with that group, which would make it hard for them to catch me alone. Although this hadn't discouraged them yet and they continued to follow the group and me everywhere that we went. At one time it appeared that the thugs had lost us and then, when I looked again, they were back.

A shuttle bus had pulled up next to the curb and I climbed on it with the group and we left. These men were on foot and I knew that there was no way that they would be able to follow the shuttle. At that moment, I took a deep breath as I didn't especially want my head smashed in, or shot from a gun that one of them had hidden in his pocket.

The group of people turned out to be tourists and the shuttle took all of us past many things. At that time, it was almost dark and every beautiful huge casino was lit up with lights. We saw the MGM Hotel and Casino, New York-New

York Hotel and Casino, The Venetian Resort Hotel and Casino, and many others. At one stop, when I knew I was safe, I got off the shuttle and called a taxi to take me back to the Mirage. My guess was that the two thugs gave up when they lost me and left the hotel.

After I paid the taxi driver and had returned to the hotel, I took an elevator up to my room. No one had seen me, so it would be a calm night of rest, which I needed.

In the morning when I woke up, I decided that I was going to try my luck at the Golden Nugget Casino. Many years ago, this was a hot spot back in my younger days and where I had met the man who taught me how to outthink the dealer and the roulette wheel. Back then, if it hadn't been for me needing to return to my hometown, I would have stayed in Vegas and made it my new home to make money, which would have been an easier way than the way that I made money in Newark.

A few years after that, I had met Jenny and was once again poor. She didn't want to live in Vegas, so we stayed where we were and at times talked about maybe moving here later. As you know, that didn't happen. When I left her, I could have come back here, but I needed to go East as I was sure that if she came after me with an attorney, she would tell them that they could find me in Las Vegas and I didn't need or want the hassle of that.

When I arrived at the Golden Nugget, I could see that nothing had changed. It was an older casino and still one that many people went to where they tried their luck on the slots, and tables. Even if they won a hundred dollars off of a slot, they thought that they had won a thousand. Because of all the money I had sitting in my pocket, and knowing that before I left here today that I would have even more, I just smiled at them. They were just there to have fun, and it didn't matter if they walked away rich or not. As for me, I was there for entertainment, but with me being a greedy con, I was there to walk away with thousands of dollars and not just a measly hundred dollars in my pocket.

That morning I did well again at not just roulette, but also blackjack. In the short amount of time that I had been in Vegas, I had made almost a million dollars, which I refused to carry around with me. Instead, I had the cash locked up in the Mirage Hotel's safe, where I would add more of what I had made today when I returned to the hotel. It was true that Vegas was addictive, and I might have been happy living out the rest of my life there, but knowing that even at the roulette table and blackjack table, a person's luck only lasts so long, I decided that like all of the other tourists that came there. It was time for me to take my money and run. If the day came when I needed more entertainment, I would be going back there, to try my hand at luck once again.

Around 7:00 p.m. I was returning to my room. With wanting to check out some night clubs and girly shows that Vegas is famous for, I called up a dating service and told them to send over not just one girl, but two. I was going to show them a really good time at the clubs, which also included me when we had returned back to my hotel room.

In a couple of hours, the women showed up, dressed in expensive clothes as I had told the dating service not to send me prostitutes as I wanted nothing but class, and that I had the money to make it good with them. That night I treated the women like royalty with nothing but the best that Vegas had to offer.

The next morning, after the women got dressed and left my room, I was going to get ready and go to another casino that I liked, which was the Plaza Hotel Casino, to see if my luck was still with me. That day I was lucky and won even more money. I was beating the odds at the roulette table and blackjack table, and no one could beat me. By late afternoon, I was once again ready to leave. When I walked out the door, in front of me were the two thugs that I had been trying to lose a couple of nights ago. There was no escaping them now, and I was stuck there to confront them.

"Hello, I see that you found me once again," I said.

"Yes, it looks that way. The other night you did outsmart

us, but now there is no escaping us," one of the thugs replied.

"What do you want from me? I did nothing wrong that night in the casino," I spoke.

"We work for the man that you sat across from in the Mirage. He is a powerful man here and has many connections. He was irate because you were the one winning so much money as he has been the top dog at the tables for years. When you walked over to play blackjack, he started getting even more upset, and when you laughed at him, he wanted nothing more than for you to be hurt or dead. He didn't care whichever came first. The girls that you took out last night also belong to him. He has many connections in Vegas, and they told him today where you were staying. From there, we followed you here. You have been so busy playing that you didn't see us in the casino. You forgot about us. We are supposed to make good on his threat to you, but this all depends on you," the other thug said.

"What do you want and what's next?" I asked.

"That depends on you. You can either buy us off or we can drag you to the alley and beat you up, or worse. We get paid well by our boss, but some extra money in our pockets won't hurt anything. We can once again tell him that you gave us the slip. He has trusted us for years, so we are sure that he will believe us, or if you refuse to do this, we can make good on his threat and our promise to mess you up. Which is it going to be?" the thug replied.

At that moment I reached into my pocket and pulled out the $500,000 that I had walked away with that day. I showed them the money and even counted it for them. Then my next words to them were.

"Is this enough?" I asked.

"That will cover it, and if you are smart, you will get in your fancy car and drive straight out of Vegas and not come back here again. Remember that our boss has eyes everywhere and he will know if you do. At that time, he will probably have a couple of different men that he owns take care of you," the thug said.

"After I get my clothes, I will be out of here, and no, I won't return again," I said, hoping that the men walked away. The truth was that I could be a fast talker when I needed to be, and if they thought that there would never be another time that I would be returning to Vegas, they had another thing coming. Someday I would return. That day was a prime example that money can buy anything. Even life if need be.

Within a couple of hours, I was in my car and leaving to return to my hometown, where I lived before and after I met Jenny. If things went wrong that day for me, I knew that there would have been a bunch of people that I had conned in Newark that would be cheering. Being a much older man, I probably wouldn't have been able to fight my way out of a paper bag, let alone them.

—8—

ENTERTAINMENT AND MORE

I was leaving Vegas, but would be back someday. From there I drove to Kingston where I had grown up, and was married to Jenny before I left her, driving East to Newark.

I had sat in the lounge chair for some time, once again reliving my life. It appeared that moving into this house didn't change my mind from thinking about my life and the choices that I had made for many years.

I was even more certain that the coin that continued to stay with me had something to do with it. Then again, I do know that with anyone, sometimes old memories have a way of sneaking into a person's mind even when it is best to leave them in the past. I needed to find a way to clear my mind from memories that I really didn't want to remember. I knew that if I couldn't, the memories might kill me someday because of all the bad choices that I knew I had made and couldn't go back to change, or should I rephrase that, and say *might* change.

All of this started the day that I visited the grave of Jenny. What magical spell did this coin have that is continuously in my pocket?

Now that I had my own home here and was an older man, I decided that it was time for me to connect with my family again. Not sure that any of my family might still be alive in the area, I felt it was the right time to find out and try to connect with them again, by letting them know why I left the way that I did and why.

A month ago, I didn't care, but because of all of my thoughts that I have had since I first drove into Apple Grove, it seemed like the right thing for me to do. I needed to find out. Kelly was under the assumption that I had been in contact with my family. Not once did she bring up any member of my family helping Jenny after I left town. As close as she was to Jenny, she would have known about this. There was no way that I could let any of my family, or anyone, know what the con artist Robert Stone is all about as my life is my own and not an open book.

Once I found out how my family was doing, I was confident that my mind would clear and I could go forward with my life without even thinking about my past, or about anybody that I once knew. This might be the secret to the coin that I had been wondering about.

I had known a man that lived not far from us for many years. He was a farmer when my father was a rancher. He would probably be in his 80s now, and I wasn't sure if he was still alive. I do remember that he always liked me when I was growing up and after. If anyone would know about my mother, father, brother and sister, it would be him as he was my father's best friend.

I had picked up a phone book the other day in town when I was thinking about buying a home here in Apple Grove. It not only had phone numbers listed of people from Apple Grove, but also those listed in other surrounding towns. This was where I would look to see if Henry Gates was still living around here.

I checked a lot of little towns in the directory. When I came to the town of Wiley, there was a Henry Gates living there. Even though with me not knowing if it was the right one, I wrote down his address anyway. Instead of calling him, tomorrow I would pay him a visit instead. He was way too old to drive here, and besides if the conversation would go bad between us, I could always get in my car and leave.

That night I slept in a new bed in my home. It felt good after years of living in motels when I left Newark. This might not be the last home that I owned, but for now it was fine.

The next morning I woke up early, and after breakfast I was going to drive to Wiley. If it turned out that the man that I knew was not the same man that was listed in the directory, it would be no big deal. The drive was around an hour long. No heavy traffic like the city and just nice country roads and highways with beautiful scenery to enjoy along the way.

I had a GPS that showed me where to turn in each little town, to get me to Henry's home. When I arrived there, it was a house in the country. It didn't look like this Henry was a farmer. After sitting in my car for a while, enjoying the country air and looking around, I walked to the front door and knocked.

"Hello, can I help you?" a younger woman asked who had answered the front door.

"Yes, you can. Is there a man that lives here by the name of Henry Gates?" I asked.

"Yes, he is my uncle. He is in the living room right now. Would you like to speak to him?" she asked.

"Yes, and thank you," I replied as I followed her down a hallway to a larger room.

When we had entered the room, she told me that sometimes Henry was hard of hearing and because of this, I might need to speak louder when I talked to him. I told her I would if I needed to, and she walked away. I walked over to Henry. He heard me coming and turned his head to where he could see me.

"Robert Stone, is that you?" Henry asked.

"Yes, Henry, It's me. I wasn't sure if you would still remember me after all of these years," I replied

"Son, I would never forget you. I have thought about you at times, wondering where you were and what you were doing," Henry spoke.

"It has been right at 30 years since I have been back here, Henry. I had my reasons for leaving when I did and wasn't sure how everyone would feel about me if they saw me again," I responded.

"Robert, everyone has reasons for doing what they do at times, and I never have been one to judge as my choices haven't always been the best. Your leaving as quick as you did came as a surprise to all of us, though," Henry said with a slight chuckle.

"I knew it would, Henry. I was young and in a bad marriage. Jenny, my wife at the time, lied to me, and I couldn't trust her after that. As you know, I have a grown son. One that I hadn't seen until the other day at his mom's grave. Jenny passed away from a blood disease and wanted to be buried in Apple Grove where she grew up. My son's name is David and he has a family of his own now. Some people would think that when I left Jenny that I was being selfish and self-centered, and others would call it the easy way out. Regardless of what anyone believes, I have no regrets for what I did," I said.

"Robert, I would never want you to explain your actions to me. You made a choice and you are the one that has to live with it for the rest of your life. Not me," Henry responded.

"Henry I am surprised that you left Kingston and your farm," I said.

"I left there around 20 years ago. My health got bad and I couldn't farm any longer, so the only thing I could do was sell my home and land. I like Wiley. Where I live is quiet and peaceful. Where have you been living all of these years?" Henry asked.

"I lived in a city called Newark, New Jersey, Henry. I made a fairly good living there and continued to stay. I worked at many jobs. I have been thinking a lot about my parents, brother and sister. Can you tell me if they are okay, and if they are still alive?" I asked.

"I have heard about Newark and it is a big city, which I am sure has plenty of job opportunities there. After you left, Robert, Jenny didn't want your parents to be a part of your son's life. She not only blamed you, but she also blamed them because they were your parents. It upset both your mother and your father, but there was nothing that they could do. Once in a while, Jenny's mother would call them and give them an update on what was going on in David's life, but after a while her calls became less frequent, and after not hearing from her for a year, your mother and father went to Jenny's home to see if they could talk to her. Jenny wouldn't let them in the door and told them that her father and mother had passed away and that David and herself didn't need them. She told them to stay away.

"That day they decided not to go back there again, even though it hurt them because they couldn't be a part of their grandson's life. They thought about you all the time and wondered if you were okay and where you were living. They also wondered why you didn't tell them goodbye. As far as I know, both of your parents are still alive, Robert. They moved to the West Coast years ago. The elevation was lower and they felt with them getting older that they would be healthier living there. After all, neither them nor I are spring chickens anymore. As for your brother, he finally found a woman that would marry him, and he lives in Arizona some place. I don't believe that he had any children of his own and as you know, he hardly wanted to see you, his sister, or your parents before you left. He was a different sort of man, and one that no one could figure out. Your sister lives in Florida. She moved there many years ago with her husband, who got a fancy job in Orlando. They like it there. So, as you can see, Robert, your family went in many different directions in life with their own choices, just like you did," Henry said.

"Thank you for the update, Henry. Do you have a phone number for my mother and father? If you do, I would love to have it so that I can tell them why I left and make arrangements to see them again. I am sorry that Jenny was so cruel to them. She was so mad at me that she took it out on them. That was not right of her to do this. As for my brother, he was always an odd duck. No one could understand his way of thinking and probably never will. My sister always had a good head on her shoulders, so I am sure that she and her husband are doing very well. Thank you, Henry, for talking with me," I said as I shook his hand.

"Robert, it was good to see you again. I wish I could give you a phone number for your parents, but over the years we kind of drifted apart. Your father will always be my best friend. When they left, they said that they would write and they didn't. At one time I did have their number, but when I moved here, I misplaced it somewhere. I will have my niece do some more looking and see if I can find it. Meanwhile, you take care of yourself and don't make yourself a stranger. I would love to see you again sooner than the last time I saw you," Henry responded once again with a chuckle.

"Thank you, Henry. I will be back again before you have time to miss seeing me. You take care of yourself as well, and if you do locate the phone number, let me know as I will give your niece my phone number," I said as I once again shook Henry's hand and turned to walked away.

Before I left that day, I did give his niece my number. I had no fear where she was concerned, and if she did find my parents' phone number, I wanted it. I then thanked her for trusting me enough to let me speak with Henry. I had found the right Henry Gates. It was time to walk out the front door of his home to once again return to my car to drive back to Apple Grove.

While driving back, I was happy that I had chosen to visit Henry Gates. When I saw him in the wheelchair, I knew that it would have been hard for him to come to Apple Grove to visit me. Because of the visit, I had found out about my family and also about how mean Jenny had treated my parents. She'd had a grudge against me and wasn't going to stop until she'd made everyone miserable that was related to me. What a sad way to live.

That day, like many days, I was driving back home to an empty house. I kept thinking about the words once again that were said to me by Henry. With some of what he had said to me, I felt like he had indicated that he, too, had done some things that he shouldn't have done and made choices that he wished that he hadn't made.

With the words that I had heard as I grew up coming from my mother as she said, "For every action, there will be a reaction," I finally, after all of these years, agreed with her and what she was trying to install in me. With everything that I had done when I took my first breath when I was born, the choices that I made for myself were my own. When I left Jenny, because of leaving her, she chose to take it out on my family. The cons that I pulled off in Newark affected a lot of innocent people and, because of my choices, I walked away with a bunch of money that I basically stole from the companies that I worked for and the people that trusted me with their money when they handed it over to me to buy shares in the stock market for them.

This I was sure was what Jenny meant by the words that she had somehow spoke to me that day I visited her grave site.

The gold coin continued to stay with me and flash. I wondered if it would continue to do this until I made things right with many people. The one person that I would never be able to explain my actions to was Jenny as she had passed away. There was no turning back the clock. It was what it was and I needed to realize that I got where I did in life because of my actions. If I wouldn't have made the choices that I did make, I would still be that poor man struggling for everything that he had. Should I regret the choices that I made and the way I lived? I had to say NO! I had lived a good life and didn't want to go backward to the struggle that I had with Jenny and before I had met her.

That night before I went to bed, I had made up my mind that in the morning I would be going back to visit Jenny's resting place once again. Before I left there, I would put the gold coin back where I had found it. I needed to see if the coin stayed there and didn't return to my pants pocket where it thought that it belonged now. My body and mind were unsettled and I needed to feel peace again. I felt like with me doing this, that was the only way that I would be able to find it.

In the morning, after I had gone to the diner to eat breakfast, I drove up the old cemetery road to Jenny's resting place. It was very hard for me to return there once again, but I felt like this was what I had to do.

This time as I stood by Jenny's resting place, I didn't hear a car coming down the road, and so I sat down by Jenny's grave on the grass to talk to her. This was what I felt like I needed to do, in order to make peace with her. My thoughts were that she would be able to hear me when I spoke to her. I started speaking as if she was just sitting there, and still alive.

"Good morning, Jenny. I came here once again to speak to you. I don't know if you can hear me, but I heard your voice and words to me loud and clear the other day. Since my last visit here, I can't seem to find the peace that I need.

"I know that for many years you wondered what happened to me and why I left you and David that night. Now it is time for me to talk to you. That night, when we returned from the restaurant and you went to a room to cry because of what I had said to you, I decided to look in your purse. I had remembered that was the place where you kept your birth control pills as you had said that you always kept them there so you wouldn't forget to take them. I needed to know in my heart that you had been respecting my wishes all along. When I looked, I saw them. The date on them was from many months before then, and you hadn't taken any of them. I felt devastated when I saw this. I realized that all you had been doing to me from our first conversation was lying to me. Maybe not just about that issue, but everything!

"You knew that I didn't want children and you said that there would be no surprises with you dropping a bomb on me, telling me that you were pregnant. At that moment I knew that I had to get away from you because I couldn't trust you any longer. Jenny, why did you choose to lie to me?

"I watched your excitement as David grew inside you for months. There was no way that I was going to take that away from you. You wanted the baby, but I didn't! The night that you went into labor, I finished packing what I wanted to take with me and I left town after seeing the attorney the next day to get the paperwork started for our divorce. Everything that involved me at that moment was signed, sealed and would be delivered after you and David were out of the hospital. I knew that I could never be a good dad to a child.

"I left town and went East to find a job and live. I am sure that you have now heard about all of the bad things that I did there in order to make a good living. If you were alive and sitting across from me, you would be saying to me that what I did was wrong and that I had made some really bad choices for myself. The truth is, Jenny, I changed when I left you. I was hurt and for many years I couldn't trust anyone and it was all because of you. My only thoughts were to con people out of as much money as I could and because of this I became greedy. The more money I had, the more I wanted! I wasn't going to stop until I had enough money to live out the rest of my life in luxury as I felt like I deserved this.

"I not only gave up you and David, I had given up my family as well. I didn't want to be found by you or them. You had destroyed me inside, and there would be no looking back for me. Then one night I met a beautiful woman by the name of Taylor. We saw places together and it wasn't long and I had found myself deeply in love with her. She felt the same way about me. I wanted to give it one more try at love and she was the one that I had chosen to do it with. We had a lot in common and she had earned my trust. After several months of seeing each other, I was prepared to ask her to marry me. She was flying in from her home state that night when the plane that she was on crashed and burst into flames. Everyone on board was killed. She was coming to see me and I was supposed to be the one that had gone to see *her*. Instead, I chose a stupid meeting over my intended visit with her. If I didn't, I might have been the one dead.

"With me thinking about this day after day, I became even more bitter than the day before. All I could think about was how I could hurt innocent people that much more. I was scamming more people and not feeling any regrets for my actions! In fact, I was enjoying it!

"I stayed with the company that I was working for, or should I say *conning* the company more, until I finally had to get out of that city. I was losing my mind! I decided that I needed to come back home and live out the rest of my life. I had more money than I would need and, being older, I knew it was time to get out while I still could.

"At the time, when I was doing this to many people, I actually believed that I had been a poor boy in a rich man's body before I left you. My mind was really messed up! It didn't matter who I hurt to get what I wanted!

"The other day when I was here, I heard what you said to me, Jenny. You told me that it was all about choices and to change and start again. There is no going back to change anything that I have done, whether it be right or wrong. For 30 years now, I chose to live my life the way that I wanted it to be, and I have no regrets inside me for anything that I chose to do.

"I'm sorry that you felt the need to hurt my parents by not letting them be a part of David's life. I knew that you would hate me, but I didn't think that you would be as cruel as you were to them. That was your choice, Jenny, and not a good one! You wanted everyone to feel sorry for you with your poor-me pity party that you had going on inside yourself, but the reality is, Jenny, that you had choices too, and you chose to lie to me, maybe more than I already know about. *Now* who is the bad person, Jenny!

"Today, I am bringing back the coin that I found on your grave the day I was here. It is forcing me to remember my entire life from the first day that I met you. I just want to live in the present now and not the past. If you wanted me to have this coin, I am giving it back to you as I feel like it belongs with you and not me.

"I have said what I came here to say to you, and I probably won't be back again. I hope that you are resting in peace, Jenny!" I said as I took the gold coin out of my pocket and placed it on top of the grass in the exact spot where I had picked it up from. I then walked away to return to my car. I believed that the coin should have stayed there, and was hoping that it didn't return to me!

My talk with Jenny took a lot out of me that day. I didn't hear her voice again. I wasn't used to going to a cemetery and sitting on the grass next to someone that was buried in the ground, spilling my guts. It had to be done, though, as Jenny needed to hear that *she* was the one who drove me away from her and not the other way around.

When I arrived back in the town of Apple Grove, I could see that the streets were closed off. There was a home town parade waiting to happen. I hadn't seen anything like this in years and was prepared to sit in my car and watch all of it.

After I had walked through my front door to my home, I was walking up the stairs to take a shower and change clothes. Later that night I was going to visit a club that I had seen not far from town. It was time to check out the night life again. I needed some female companionship once again, and that was a good place to go to find it.

As I emptied my pockets before putting them with the other dirty clothes, I once again saw that the gold coin had come back to me! I wasn't sure why it was so attached to me, and even taking it back to where I had found it didn't help. This was starting to creep me out even more than before, and now I was wondering if Jenny was trying to drive me crazy from her grave!

I was more confused than I had ever been in my life. I had heard about supernatural occurrences happening all of the time and chose not to believe that something this bizarre could happen to anyone, let alone me. I had tried for days to come up with a solid reason why this kept happening to me, and I couldn't come up with anything that made any sense.

The only thing that I did know was that, for some reason, this coin wanted to be with me and not with Jenny, and that maybe this was the reason why it kept turning up in the pocket of my pants every day.

As for tonight, my plans were still in motion. I would forget about the coin as it hadn't done anything to me other than scare the living daylights out of me thinking that it was some kind of a voodoo coin or maybe a supernatural existence that flashed off and on at times. I had no idea what Jenny did when I left her or what kind of clubs and organizations she had chosen to be a part of. Maybe she had turned into a witch of some sort. The thought of that made me laugh and all I could do was stand there in the middle of my bedroom, naked, and say, "No that isn't possible, or is it?"

After I set the coin on the dresser and told it that I would be back to get it shortly after I took a shower and changed clothes, I was laughing again. Now I was talking to a coin and this would be too funny to try to explain to anyone.

I showered and got dressed. I put everything I had set on the dresser back in my pants pocket. Tonight I was dressed in an expensive suit and I looked like I was worth a million dollars. The truth be known, I was—and maybe more if I checked my bank account again.

I was needing some excitement in my life to take my mind in a different direction. I knew that a couple of women would be entertainment enough for me that night. I had called the most expensive motel in Brighton and made reservations for the night for me and whomever wanted to come back there with me. There was no way that they would ever know my real name or where I really lived. Once a con artist, always a con artist.

I locked my front door to my house. Brighton was a distance away, so it would take me awhile to get there. My only thought was that I hoped that I didn't see Kelly that night as she lived in that town. It was party time again for me. With me not drinking any alcohol, I had learned how to have fun without getting loaded and then not remembering anything of what I had done the night before that next day. This was something that a lot of people couldn't understand as they always thought that they had to drink to have fun. I never did, and I know that I had more fun than they ever did.

When I drove away, I was sure that night out on the town would give me some peace that I really needed in my life right now. I had a fancy Mercedes Benz and wanted to show it off to everyone that I saw. When I left Kingston many years ago, I drove an older pickup truck that needed new tires before the winter months arrived. What a difference 30 years and lots of money can make.

I was glad that I had visited Jenny one last time. I didn't know for sure if she actually heard anything that I said to her as she laid motionless in her grave, but a part of me believed that she did, as why else would she have talked to me the first day that I had visited her resting place!

I was ready for a night of fun and on my way to find it. Within a half hour, I was inside the club, checking out not just the women that were in there, but the club itself. I was only used to high class places like Newark and Vegas, and I was dressed nicer than any man in there. The women were checking me out as well, and it wasn't long before I spotted a couple of women that were also dressed nicely, sitting at a table. These two women looked like maybe they actually might have some decent jobs, and weren't there to pick up a man, unlike the other women that I had noticed. I wanted class when I went in there, and not trash!

I walked over to their table and sat down beside them. I told them that I was in town on business and was from Newark. I also asked them what they did for a living. One of the women told me that she was an accountant and the other one said that she was a nurse that worked in the local hospital. I noticed that neither one of them were drinking alcohol. This was more of a turn-on for me than I'd had for quite some time. I told them that I was there for the night and partially the next day. Also, that if they would like to come with me, I would take them to an expensive restaurant, where we could eat, and then to a musical if they liked. I told them that if they chose to come back to the motel with me, that I would love to just sit and talk, and hopefully get to know them.

Well, this didn't turn out very good, as the ladies said that what I had just offered them sounded very boring, and that they came there looking for more excitement than that. I then told them that I had more money than they could ever dream about, and that if they were looking for that kind of a good time that I would pay them for their time. They knew what I was talking about and this seemed to work, as one of the women stood up out of her chair and said, "What are we waiting for?"

The other one got up as well and stood at the table looking at me. I then stood up and said, "Ladies, let's go have some real fun." They both smiled at me, and we walked out of the club, arm in arm. There was no beating around the bush for me that night, and at my age now, that was maybe a good thing.

From the club we went back to a fancy restaurant where I had told them to order whatever they wanted to eat. After we had eaten we left, and in the car as we were driving, they both told me that they were ready to make some money in my motel room. This was easier than I thought.

When we got in the room, I was ready for a good time, but instead, one of the women gave me a sob story about how she had a child that needed a bunch of medical attention, and the other woman agreed that she also had a kid that depended on her for help. It wasn't the fact that they had told me that they had kids, as that was their thing, and after the night I would never see them again, so that part didn't matter to me. What really made me curious was the timing of the conversation, and waiting until they were in the motel room with me. I felt like I at that moment had been played like a sucker, and that these women were not who they were pretending to be, so the red flags were put in place where they were concerned.

I told them that I decided that I was too tired for any entertainment and that I would mail them a check. They became irate, and that night I got called words that I hadn't heard in a long time. Then they left. I sat there, thinking for a while, wondering if they were actually undercover cops that were pretending to be an accountant and a nurse, waiting at the right moment to pull a badge out when I took off my clothes for entertainment. They might even be high-class prostitutes who were trying to make more money for their boss. Whatever or whoever they were didn't get very far with me, and a con can spot another con. The most money that I had spent on them was buying them dinner. There was no way that they could arrest me for that! This made me laugh once again.

I was ready to return to the club again. This time I made sure that the kind of women that came with me were just in it for a good time and nothing more. The next morning, the two women found a little something lying next to them on the bed for them to have when they woke up. I had left the motel and was on my way back home.

When I walked through my front door, I took my overnight bag upstairs to unpack. After I had finished, I reached in my pocket to see if the coin was still with me. Today the coin was flashing more than it had flashed before, and I wasn't sure what was going on with it. I laid down in bed to rest for a while. The entertainment that I had the night before had made me realize that I wasn't as young as I used to be. As I laid there, I started thinking about what my life might have been like if I had taken it in a different direction.

Vegas is a nice city, and like I had mentioned before, I could have made a bunch of money living and working there. I just needed to know when to walk away from the roulette and blackjack table before my luck went bad and I lost everything. I could have become a rancher like my father was at the time, but there was a risk in that as well. Some years the beef prices were higher than other years, and the money that I had made one year might not be as good the next year, or years to come. I could have gone to college after high school like my sister did, and actually gotten a degree in business like I had told the bosses of the different companies that I worked for in Newark that I had. I could have not married Jenny and found someone else.

There was so much going on in my mind at that time. It was becoming more unsettled every day. After I had laid there thinking for a while, I drifted off to sleep. I don't know how long I had been sleeping when I saw Jenny, David, Kelly and Taylor standing in front of my bed. My dream was so real, and at one point in the dream I thought that I was actually awake.

This was when I asked, "What are all of you doing here?" I was so confused. Jenny and Taylor were dead, and David wouldn't give me the time of day. Kelly wasn't sure if she believed what I told her, or if I made it all up to make myself look good and Jenny a bad person when I left her. I remember laying there and thinking that I had to have woken up, and then thinking that there was no way that I could have. Jenny still looked the same as she did when I had left her and that wasn't possible!

All four of them were screaming at me at once, and during this time I looked at all of them as their words that they spoke to me were very loud and clear.

"What do you think we are doing here, Robert?" Jenny screamed

"You are dead, Jenny! How could you be here?" I spoke loudly.

"What kind of a father leaves his wife and newborn son!" David said as he yelled those words, pointing his finger at my face.

"I told you that I had no regrets, David! Your mother lied to me!" I said in a harsh tone.

"Robert, I don't think that I can believe you. Jenny is my

best friend!" Kelly loudly spoke.

"I don't care if you believe me or not! I was telling you the truth!" I yelled out at Kelly.

"Robert, why did you choose money over me? I should still be alive," Taylor said with anger in her voice.

"You are right, Taylor! I should have been the one that was killed and not you! I loved you!" I said with tears in my eyes.

"We are always going to be with you, Robert! I told you that it is all about choices and changes and to start again, Robert!" Jenny screamed back at me.

"Go away, Jenny! I have no regrets for what I did!" I shouted back at her.

"You will never be my father, and don't ever call me your son!" David said again as he yelled at me.

"What kind of a man are you, Robert? You should have never wanted me to choose between you and Jenny!" Kelly said loudly.

"NO, Kelly, I would have never wanted you to choose between me and Jenny! I just wanted you to hear my side of the story!" I said with anger in my voice.

"You should have been the one on that plane that night, and not me!" Taylor yelled out.

"I know, Taylor! You should still be alive!" I said with more tears running down my face.

The more they spoke, their words started to run together as all four of them were screaming at me, telling me what they had to say, and their faces were getting closer to mine. By then they were standing close to each other and closer to me! They kept coming closer and closer, and I was telling them to leave me alone as this was just a bad dream. Even with those words to them, they were right in front of my face and I could feel sweat pouring off of me. I kept trying to get out of bed and run, but I couldn't. My legs wouldn't move.

By then I was looking at the gold coin and screaming, crying, and saying the words, "TAKE ME BACK IN TIME! GET ME OUT OF HERE NOW!"

At that moment, the gold coin turned brighter and brighter, and when I opened my eyes, I was lying in the same bed that I had slept in every night when I was 14 years old in my mother and father's house! I looked around the room and wondered how I had gotten here! I was having many emotions and one of them was fear! I was wearing clothes that I had worn when I was 14 years old, and my old room still looked the same.

I reached in my pocket to see if the gold coin was still there with me, and it was! It had taken me back in time to live parts of my life again, to try to change the bad choices that I had made in my life. The coin at that time wasn't flashing and was dim. I put it back in my pocket and laid there, wondering where it was going to take me next whenever it thought the right time would be.

I still had my same thoughts in my mind. I still remembered what I had done with my life before I came back here. The coin was giving me a chance to redo the choices that I had chosen for myself, and change my life to the right way that it should have been all along. I knew that some of what I had done I wouldn't be able to change, but maybe I could make things right with many people, and this is why the gold coin wouldn't leave me. I had to tell it to take me back in time and that I didn't want to be there any longer. The reason why it stayed with me was clear to me now!

As I laid on my bed, I heard my mother calling me for dinner. "Robbie, come eat. It's on the table," Mother said.

"Okay, Mother," I said as I got up from my bed. My voice was the same as when I was 14, and I kept thinking about the words from other people saying, "If only I could go back in time and change some things that I did wrong." I had that opportunity to do this and would try hard to make good choices this time, to try to undo the damage that I had done for years to many people.

I knew that some things I wouldn't be able to change, like Jenny passing away from a blood disease, but it was obvious to me now that I could change the choices that I had chosen for myself if I wanted to, and could change the direction of my life.

When I entered the kitchen and sat down in my chair, I saw my father walking through the front door and going to the sink to wash his hands to get ready to eat. My mother and father were both very young and my dog, Alex, was even there, lying next to me on the kitchen floor. It was warm outside and I could see that it was summer, and soon Father would be asking me to go with him to the pasture to help feed the livestock. I was young again and ready for this experience again and being able to hang out, not just with my father, but also with my mother, sister and brother.

"Where's Carl? Don't tell me that his car broke down on him again!" Father said.

"Carl will be here later, Tom. He has a date tonight. They are going to see a picture show," Mother replied.

"I swear, that boy is useless, Karen! He always manages to have some kind of an excuse to get out of helping me feed the cows and horses. I don't know what he is going to do after high school and he is out of this house and on his own!" Father commented with anger in his voice.

"Now Tom, you know that Carl is a teenager. The only thing he thinks about right now is girls. I am sure that he will do just fine after high school," Mother replied with a smile on her face.

Mother was always sticking up for all three of us kids. Father, on the other hand, was not. He could see that Carl was different than my sister Pam and I were, and I always wondered why Mother refused to see it for herself. How little did they both know that when he did grow up, he would have a hard time keeping a job with him getting fired from many of them because he kept chasing after the wrong kind of women. Later in life, Mother would find out that Father knew more than she thought he did.

"Now that we have discussed why Carl isn't here with us sitting at this table eating with us, what is Pam's excuse for not being here?" Father asked Mother.

"Pam has to work tonight, Tom. Her boss has her scheduled to close down the soda fountain at 9:00. She will be here, but a little later," Mother spoke, hoping that Father would change the subject of wanting to just talk about Carl, and Pam.

Later in life, Pam was the one that went to college and made something of her life. She wouldn't settle for anything less than the best. Kind of like the choices that I had made for myself. The only difference was that Pam did it the honest way, unlike me.

"Well, I guess that leaves you and me, son, to go out and feed the livestock after we eat. You are just about the only one that I can count on," Father commented as he smiled at me.

"I would be happy to help you do this, Father," I replied back to him.

At that moment I realized that Father depended on me a lot during the years that I was growing up. I watched him and Mother struggle some years to put food on the table and pay bills. He couldn't afford a ranch hand to help him, and so he chose me. I guess that is why I had decided not to take up ranching when I grew up. I wanted more out of life and had seen the sweat that poured off of my father's face at times from working by himself when he had to be outside with the hot sun beating down on him.

That night after we had all of the chores done, Father and Mother went to bed. I was 14 and still awake when my sister Pam came home. Pam was 17 and Carl was 16. Pam, being more responsible than Carl, knew that someday she would find the right man in life and that she didn't need to cruise up and down the streets in town, looking for a boy to take her out on a date. She was very smart and very pretty. Carl, on the other hand, was okay to look at, but he had a hard time finding a date, and when he did, he always did something to mess up any kind of a relationship with the girl.

I was tired from being outside and helping Father feed

all of the cows and horses that we had, so I went back to my room to sleep, wondering if the flashing coin would allow me to still be here in the morning.

Pam, on the other hand, stayed up to wait for Carl to return. She was the big sister that worried about Carl and me. Especially Carl tonight as she knew where I was.

In the morning when I woke up and opened my eyes, I looked around and I was still laying in my old bed. My thoughts were that it wasn't time for the coin to take me on another journey as there was more to learn about why I had turned out the way that I was and made some of the choices that I had later made in life. I could hear Mother working in the kitchen and smelled food cooking on the stove. She was once again preparing breakfast for all of us. I put on my bathrobe and went to the kitchen.

"Good morning, Robbie. How did you sleep?" Mother asked.

"I slept better than I have in a long time, Mother. How did you sleep?" I replied

"That's good, son. I slept okay. Your father tossed and turned a lot last night, but finally he settled down. That gave me the opportunity to fall asleep. What are your plans today? You only have one more week before school starts up again," Mother said.

"I don't know yet, Mother. I thought that I might have Pam take me into town for a while today. I haven't seen much of my friends this summer. If I see any of them, I will ask them if they would like to go with me to the high school. Today is the day that we register and choose what classes we want to take this year in school," I remarked.

"I am sure that Pam won't mind doing this as she is scheduled at the drugstore to work an earlier shift today. If Carl isn't awake when you leave, would you please wake him up? I have some chores for him to help me with," Mother spoke.

"Yes, I will be happy to do this for you. I am not sure what time he got home last night as I went to bed not long after you and Father did," I responded.

"Father is right, you know," Mother said.

"Right about what?" I asked.

"You, Robbie, are the most reliable son that we have. We both know that we can count on you for anything and everything," Mother replied with a smile on her face.

I looked at Mother and thanked her for what she had just said. I wanted to cry as I knew that with the choices that I had chosen for myself in life, that both she and Father would never have been proud of me again if they knew about me being a con artist after I left Jenny and Kingston.

I managed to wake up Carl at around noon as he liked to sleep late. This was a big reason why he couldn't keep a job. Father had already given up on his help, and was in the pasture tending to the livestock. Pam was getting ready to walk out the door to go to work, and I caught her in time to get a ride into town. So far, my day was going well. I once again reached in my pocket to see if the coin was still with me. It was there.

After Pam had dropped me off in town, she went to work. I started walking toward the high school in hopes of seeing some of my friends. It wasn't long and Mike had spotted me. Mike was kind of a cocky kid that the girls in my class loved. He came from a richer family than I did, but he still at times liked to hang around me, even with me coming from a poor family. I kind of admired him because he knew what he wanted and went after it. I was a shy boy back then that had a lot of growing to do. There were times when I thought that I would like to be more like Mike than the way I was. Maybe this is why I had a huge ego when I grew up and a cocky attitude, and when I left Jenny, it became even worse. I had been around Mike enough that I knew that he was a fast talker, and loved the girls like my brother Carl did. The only difference was that Mike knew how to play them, and my brother Carl had many years to learn how to do that.

"Rob, where are you going?" Mike asked

"I am going to the school. Today is the day that we are

supposed to register and pick our classes. I thought that you knew about this. Do you want to come with me?" I asked.

"Yes, I'll tag along with you for a while. Maybe we will see some hot chicks along the way that will want to hang out with us tonight," Mike said with a slight giggle.

"Tonight, Mike I need to help my father with the livestock. I am the only one that he has to help him. My brother Carl is useless, according to my father," I spoke.

"Okay Rob. You choose whatever you want to do, but if you change your mind, I will be hanging around town for most of the day until I need to return home," Mike replied.

At that time, Mike made up a lame excuse why he would go to the high school later in the day, and left me standing there. That was fine. I kind of expected Mike to not want to hang around me that long as at that time we were two different people and his personality was different than mine. After I left Jenny, I wanted to be more like Mike in my mind. A *player* was what he was, and because of his ego, and the money that he knew he could have anytime he wanted it, he considered himself a lady's man. Somewhere inside me at that time, after I left Jenny from feeling betrayed, I had already decided that this was the way that I wanted to live *my* life. Now the choice was mine, whether I wanted to change it or stay the same.

I had registered at the school and caught a ride back to the house with Pam after she was done with work. When we walked through the front door, we both overheard Mother and Father arguing, and so we just stood there, not knowing whether to leave or stay put.

"Tom, I am sorry that you feel the way that you do! I know that we can't afford another mouth to feed, but we are being blessed with another child!" Mother told father.

"I don't care, Karen. You should have made sure that this didn't happen! I don't want any more kids. We have enough right now. We are barely making ends meet this year, and I can't guarantee what next year is going to bring. The meat prices might be down even more, and if this happens, no one is going to be buying beef! I can sell some horses if I need to, in order to pull us through this rough patch, but this is all that I can do! I can't help the way that I feel about you being pregnant, Karen! When I took over this ranch when my father passed away, I told you at that time that I wasn't ready for kids as we were struggling back then. Instead, you ended up pregnant with Pam, and then a year later we had Carl, and then Robert. I love all of them, Karen, and you know this, but I wasn't ready for a family yet! In fact, I wasn't sure if I would even be a good father to them! I won't ask you to give up this baby, Karen, as I am sure you love the fact that you are going to be a mother again, but I am not happy with this at all!" Father spoke loudly to Mother.

I heard Father's words, and the way he felt stuck in my mind, and at the age of 14 his words managed to form my way of thinking. This was why I didn't want children, and why I felt the need to run when David was being born. Jenny and I were struggling and couldn't afford another mouth to feed, like Mother and Father couldn't. Now that was very clear to me. As far as I knew, Pam didn't have any children either, so this must have made an impact on her as well! As for Carl, I hadn't seen him in so many years, and with him not being there at that time, hearing Father's words that he spoke, he probably still wanted children or already had fathered many of them.

After Father had finished yelling at Mother, Pam and I pretended like we had just gotten there, and when we sat down to eat dinner, Mother and Father were very quiet. We both looked at each other and knew the reason why.

That night like I always did in the past, I went out to help Father feed the livestock. I could see that his face was strained, and after hearing what I did, I knew why. He was trying to figure out in his mind what he would choose to do. Once again, Carl came home late with a lame excuse as Father would have put it, and went straight to bed. It wasn't long after that when Pam and I also called it a night and went to our rooms to sleep.

In the morning I once again woke up in my own bed. It was another day for me to find out if there was another reason why I chose the path that I had taken. This day could be interesting and probably why I had a trust issue going on when I grew up as at that time Father felt betrayed, like I did with Jenny.

Several months had passed and I was still there with the gold coin still sitting in my pants pocket. Pam and I could see that Mother and Father, at that time, were straying away from each other. They still were talking, but not as much. Father chose to be outside more, working, as Mother stayed extra busy in the kitchen. Mother was very pregnant and at times she would rub her stomach and smile. Whether Father wanted to have more children didn't matter to her as she had already felt her baby kick and loved it even more than she did when the doctor first told her that she was going to be a mother again. Father could see this as I could see it on Jenny's face, and he didn't smile or want to feel the baby moving or kicking in Mother.

Pam and I knew that this was hurting Mother, but there was nothing that we could do about it. I, on the other hand, hung out with Father more and at times he would tell me that he didn't think he was a good father to me, Pam or Carl, and that he didn't really want to be a father again to another child. With all of his words and actions, I am sure this is why I behaved the way that I did where Jenny was concerned. It took me coming back in time to relive the different moments that were occurring, to make me understand some of why I chose to be the way that I am and have been. I had forgotten over time all of this or I had just put it out of my mind.

One morning, when Father had gone out to the pasture and Pam and Carl had gone to school, I noticed that Mother didn't feel well. She was sitting in her chair at the kitchen table when I entered the room. She looked very pale and was holding her stomach. I questioned her on how she felt and told her that she didn't look like her normal self. Mother told me that she would be fine and for me to go ahead and leave so that I wouldn't miss the school bus.

I picked up my books and told her that I would be back home right after school, and that I hoped by then that she felt better. Mother then said that everything always works out the way that it is supposed to in our lives and for me not to spend my day worrying about her. I told her that I wouldn't, but the truth was that I couldn't help but worry.

That afternoon when I did arrive back home, there was a strange car sitting in the yard. I was not familiar with this car and thought at the time that maybe Mother or Father was just having a visit from a friend. When I entered the house, I saw Father talking to whom I found out later to be Mother's doctor. Father had a sad look on his face, and the doctor as well. Mother had gone into early labor and lost the baby that she was carrying.

I knew that there was a part of Father that felt relieved as he, for many months, was dreading the day that the baby was born, and because of this he was staying away from Mother more and more, so that she wouldn't see this happening with him. Finally, the doctor left and Father went in the bedroom to talk to Mother. By then, Pam had returned home and I told her what I thought maybe had happened. We both felt very badly for Mother, but there was nothing that we could do to change it.

As for Carl, he continued to spend most of his time when he wasn't in school chasing around after girls and he continued most of his life doing this. Pam nor I could really get close to him as he chose to stay away from all of us and pretty much shut us out of his life.

So many things were making sense to me now and I was learning more and more about why I chose to be the way that I am and was after I grew up.

More months passed and by then, Mother was speaking to Father again and they looked more content with each other than they had been. I could see from time to time pain in Mother's eyes as she really wanted the baby that she had been carrying. I think this was why I worked extra hours when Jenny almost lost David and had to be on bed rest. I wanted her to have her child, even though I didn't want it. The missing puzzles of my life were coming together for the first time in many years.

That night, before I went to sleep, I once again reached in my pants pocket to see if the coin was still with me like I did every day. It was, so I turned off my light and went to sleep.

In the morning when I woke up, I wasn't that 14-year-old boy again. Now I was 16 years old and wearing the same clothes once again that I had worn back then. Carl was 18 and getting ready to graduate from high school. Pam had graduated the year before, and at that time she was still living at home. Before long she would be leaving to travel to the college where she had gotten accepted. As for Carl, I think all of us were wondering how he even was graduating from high school.

Father's best friend, Henry Gates, had once again stopped by to visit. He, too, was a very young man, and my father and Henry would sit for hours talking about many things. Mother thought a lot of Henry as well and would always invite him to eat dinner with us.

That night was graduation and all of us were dressed up in our nicest clothes, going to the school to watch Carl receive his diploma. When he walked up on the stage, of course we clapped for him. Even though Carl would have been happier missing graduation and cruising up and down the main street of town looking for girls, with this he looked like he was happy to be out of school now and did smile when the diploma was handed to him.

By the time we got back to the house, it was late and time to go to bed. The next morning Carl informed Mother and Father that he was going to pack his stuff as he and his friend were leaving town and going elsewhere to find a job. Of course, Father and Mother told him that they wished him well and that they hoped he found what he was looking for. At that time, I am sure that the only thing they were thinking was that this, hopefully, would be a good thing, and be what caused him to make changes in his life. As far as I know, he stayed the same way for many years. We hardly heard from him, and when we did, he was calling to let us know that he was with a different woman and still looking for work. Pam and I also hugged him goodbye and told him that we would miss him. Once again, the truth was that we hardly saw him when he reached a certain age anyway, as he was always gone from the house.

More months went by and I was still 16. At that time, I too, was driving, and once in a while would ask Mother and Father if I could hang out with my friends. They both were okay with it as they knew that I was nothing like Carl and would always help them first if need be. That one night that I chose to hang out with Mike and a couple more of my friends turned into something that I didn't expect.

Mike was still the same. His ego had enlarged even more than it had before, and he still had lots of girls chasing after him. He didn't care how he treated them, and whether he hurt anyone at all as long as it got him where he needed to be and what he wanted. This was just one more piece of the puzzle that had come together for me, because even though I knew that he was wrong in being the way he was and doing what he did, there was still a part of me that had learned a lot from him that also stuck in my mind. The only one he continued to care about was himself.

That night when we were cruising around on Main Street, Mike saw a parked car that didn't have a driver in it. He wanted to stop his car so that all of us could get out and take a look inside of this really nice car. He pulled over to the curb, and when we walked to the car, Mike said, "Look at this! No driver, but the keys are still there. How about all of us taking it for a ride? I will drive and we can cruise Main and check out all the girls, and then see if any of them want to ride around with us."

I tried to talk him out of it as I wasn't sure if the owner would be back soon. When he saw that his car was missing, he would involve the police. With Mike being like I turned out to be, he had sold me on the idea, saying that we would not get into trouble and if we got stopped, he would do the talking.

We drove for about an hour and then a police car pulled up behind us with his lights on, and Mike had to pull over to the side of the street. When the policeman walked up to the car, Mike did the talking and said that he thought the car belonged to his uncle, who wouldn't care if he took it for a ride, and how he was sorry if it wasn't his uncle's car.

The police officer, seeing that all of us were minors, told us to get out of the car and he would call for someone to come there to pick it up. We piled out and were also informed that we would need to call our parents. This was something that I really didn't want to do as my parents had so much faith in me and believed that I was such a perfect boy, and I didn't want them to know about this.

It wasn't long and my parents, along with all the other parents, showed up to get each one of us to take us home. Mother and Father said that it was late and that they would talk to me about what I had done in the morning. I knew that they weren't happy with me for that choice that I had made that night.

As I laid in bed, I remembered all the lies that I told after I moved away from Jenny and David, and how I became a good con artist who didn't care whom he hurt in the process. I was a player and loved to play anyone who would let me, or believe me. This I am sure was because I hung around Mike. He was bad for me, but because I was shy growing up, Mike had taught me what I thought I needed to know later on in life. This, unfortunately, was how to lie, steal, cheat and deceive others.

—9—

MIND OF ITS OWN

The next morning, when I opened my eyes and realized that I was still there at the old house in my own bed, I knew that Father and Mother would be waiting for me in the kitchen. I was sure that I was in a bunch of trouble with them and at that time wasn't sure what to expect.

Thinking back on my entire life after I grew up and all the bad decisions that I had made, I was sure that when I saw Mother and Father that they would have a lecture for me. My thoughts now were why their lecture didn't stick with me after I grew up. As I thought about it longer, the only reasoning that I could come up with stemmed once again around Jenny and all the manipulations and lies that she had told me, not to mention done to me. Before I met her, I was a trusting man. After she threw me under the bus mentally, I gave myself permission to change and become like Mike.

I hesitated to get out of bed and I thought that if I laid there long enough, the coin would magically take me to a different segment of my life and I wouldn't have to see the disappointment on Mother's and Father's faces when I entered the kitchen.

It wasn't long after thinking this when Mother came into my room.

"Are you awake, Robbie?" Mother asked softly.

"Yes, Mother. I'm awake," I replied.

"Please come into the kitchen so that you can eat some breakfast and your father can talk to you," she commented.

"Okay, Mother, I will be in there in a minute," I said, thinking at the time that when I got in there and sat down that I was in a huge amount of trouble.

Mother left my room and I sat up, putting on my slippers, and bathrobe. I was going in there to face the music, no matter what was said to me. I wasn't excited about getting a lecture, even though I knew that I deserved it. I walked out of my bedroom and into the kitchen.

When the coin took me back in time, it had wiped out my memory of my childhood as it wanted me to live my life again the way that it was back then, showing me what had made me the man that I had become in my older years and why. My memory of my older life and the way I was, and am now, had stayed with me. So I was a younger me with an older mind that had lived many years prior to that day.

"Good morning," Father said.

"Good morning, Father," I replied, wondering what was next.

"That was quite the night that you had last night. Do you have anything to say for yourself?" Father asked.

"I can't make an excuse for what I did, Father, as I already know that I was wrong going along with what Mike wanted to do. Mike and I have been friends since we started school together. Some way with me knowing how he is, I have looked up to him. I have always been his shy friend. Mike has always known what he wanted and went after it, no matter what the cost. I knew better than to get in that car with him and my other two friends, but I went ahead and did it anyway. Whatever your punishment is that you and Mother feel that I deserve, I will accept it as I know that I deserve it," I spoke.

"You are getting older, son. Your mother and I know this as we were young ourselves once. Sometimes every one of us finds ourselves in the wrong situations, and we believe that this is what happened to you last night. All we want you to do is to think about what could have gone wrong. If Mike would have caused an accident or you could have been in one, you would have been just as accountable as he was for it. We aren't going to punish you this time as we already know how good of a person you are and that from now on you will think before you act to any situation," Father spoke.

Father and Mother had raised me right and I did know right from wrong. That day I was expecting the worst and it had turned out okay. My father was a forgiving man and my mother was a forgiving woman. The day that I skipped town on Jenny and David, I should have gone to their home and talked to them about it first. My choice might have been the same way as I have no way of knowing now how it would have turned out, but if I would have done this, I wouldn't have lost all of the years that I did with my family.

Mother brought Father and me breakfast, and until we left the house to go outside to feed the animals, we sat there eating and laughing about many situations that my father shared with me about his bad choices in life. I had seen a different side to him and this was something that I was looking for since the day that I was born. He wasn't the sober-faced man that I had seen so many times. That was when I knew that my father not only had a sense of humor, but that he could be understanding as well. I always felt close to him before that moment, but today I felt even closer.

After we ate breakfast, we went out in the pasture and I once again helped him take care of the livestock. When it started getting dark, we went back to the house to wash our hands and get ready for dinner. Mother had a big pot of stew waiting for us as she knew that we were going to be hungry when we sat down to eat.

That night I went to bed at the same time that they did. Pam was gone, like Carl, and they were where they wanted to be in their life and I knew that they weren't coming home.

When the sun shone through my window the next day, I woke up. This time, though, I had gone from being 16 years old to the age of 23. I guess the coin thought that I had learned everything that I needed to learn about myself being a kid and what had led up to some of the choices that I had made, and decided to bump me up in age.

In a way I felt sad as I could have stayed there, being a kid forever, enjoying my mother's cooking as she always prepared great meals every day, and helping my father in the barn and pasture with the livestock. Life was so much easier back then, and at that time I hadn't made the choices that I did after I left Jenny.

This morning I was laying in the same bed in the apartment where I had lived before I met Jenny and where we had lived before I left. I was back working for the same construction company where I had worked before I had left Kingston. At that time, I was still a trusting and nice guy.

That day I had gone to work to learn that my mother had called to talk to me. Mother and Father were coming there to bring me an old quilt that had belonged to my grandmother, who had just passed away. I saw them drive up when I was working out in the company yard, and walked over to their car to talk to them. We talked for a few minutes and they had invited me to eat dinner with them on Sunday after they got back from church. I was happy to do this as, like I said, my mother was a great cook. Also, it would give me time to spend with them when I wasn't working, and also time that I loved helping Father feed the cows and horses. I told them that I needed to get back to work and would see them on Sunday. They both smiled and drove away.

That night was the night that I was supposed to meet Jenny for the first time. Even with a coin directing my life, I knew the exact date and time that I had met her 31 years ago. I wasn't sure that I wanted to take that path in life again. I liked the restaurant where she worked, but my thoughts were still the same on not wanting any children. So, I came up with a plan. One that I was sure would work. I asked a friend of mine from work named Allen Strout if he would like to go out that night and have some fun. I told him that we could eat at that restaurant and that I was sure that he would love the food. He told me that he knew exactly which one I was talking about, and that he had eaten there before. He agreed to go with me, and this was going to be the first course that would change the bad choices that I had made before and after I left Jenny. I do know that in some way Jenny was supposed to be a part of my life and that what I did with our friendship was on me.

So that night, after Allen and I had entered the restaurant, I started walking over to the same table that I sat at when Jenny was walking past me the night we met. Allen followed me. If things were the same as years ago, Jenny would be going in the same direction as she did that night. This time I sat down in a different chair and the only one left was the one that I had sat in 31 years ago. Allen sat down in it, and the plan was set and ready to happen. It wouldn't be long and Jenny would be walking past Allen, only to slip on water that had been spilled on the floor. Before long, Allen would be the one wearing the hot coffee and food, and not me. That night I would stay dry as a bone.

At the exact moment I saw Jenny walking our way. I told Allen that I would be back as I had seen a guy that I knew and I needed to tell him something. I got up from my chair and walked away, only to hide around the corner of the hall leading to the restrooms, to watch the show that was getting ready to take place.

When Jenny was behind Allen, she once again slipped. In the process of her falling, she spilled hot coffee and food on Allen and herself. Allen was a little upset as I was that night, but he stood up like I had and picked Jenny up. Just like before, when this had happened to me and Jenny, as we stood there laughing at how we both looked. This was a repeat of the past with a different man. This time Allen was the man that would take my place in Jenny's life and be David's father. I always thought that Allen was a great man, but not as great a man as my father.

I had given them a chance to talk and Jenny a chance to walk away, and then I went back to the table. Allen told me what had happened to them and, of course, I said, "Oh yeah?" I wanted to act ignorant to the fact that I had already played that part and once was enough for me.

We sat there and ate, and every so often Allen would smile at Jenny as she would smile at him.

This went on the whole evening as we stayed at the restaurant for some time, eating and talking. After a couple of hours, we left. Allen went to his place where he lived, and I had returned to my dingy, tiny apartment to sleep. I was feeling good about what I had done that night.

In the morning when I woke up once again, I expected to be in a different place, but the coin must have thought that I needed to stay in that time period longer. It was the weekend, and if my guess was right, when I went to the restaurant again tonight to eat at the exact time that I had gone before many years ago, I would see Allen sitting at that table, talking and flirting with Jenny as I had done. I had promised myself that I was going to somehow find a way back to Taylor and try my hardest to change the course of time there, if the coin would only let me. Taylor was the one that I had really fallen in love with and wanted to be with the rest of my life.

That day, once again I made a trip out to the ranch to help my father. We had become great friends as well as father and son, and he was a much older man. It was harder for him to do things by himself when I had left home, and at times I was there to help Mother as well. I was liking my life and felt good about the way it was working out.

When I arrived at the ranch, I saw Pam there. She had come back to Mother and Father's home to visit for a few days before she left to drive back to the city where she was living. At that time Pam was single and loving it. She had found a good job and was also liking the city that she was living in. She had completed college.

"Pam, how nice to see you!" I said.

"Robbie, it is great seeing you again. How are you doing? Are you still into construction work?" she asked.

"Yes, I am still working construction and liking it. I had no idea that you were going to be here as well. How long are you going to be here?" I asked.

"I only have a few days, but knowing me, I will make the best of the time that I am back here. Mother told me that you will be here tomorrow for dinner. I can't wait to catch up more with you on how your life is going," Pam spoke.

"I'm sure that you will see a lot of the friends that you had in school. There are many of them that stayed behind and found jobs here. As for now, I need to go help Father feed the animals, so I will see you tomorrow night," I said as I hugged her goodbye and left the house. I worked until almost dark with Father and then I went back to my apartment to change clothes. I had a date with myself watching Allen and Jenny, and this was something that I wasn't going to miss.

When I walked through the restaurant door, I could see that Jenny was talking to Allen and smiling at him. It wouldn't be long and he, too, would be asking her out on a date. It would be funny to see if there was a new twist added to this saga. I couldn't wait.

After Jenny walked away and Allen was looking around the room, he spotted me sitting at a different table quite a ways away. I had an older waitress that was more experienced and didn't spill coffee or food on me, and that was the way I liked it. Allen waved at me to come over to the table. I stood up and walked over there.

"Rob, it's good to see you here tonight. Would you like to join me?" Allen asked.

"No, but thank you. I am meeting someone here tonight and I have already ordered my food. I will catch up with you on Monday. Have a good night," I said.

"Thanks, Rob, for bringing me here last night. If you hadn't, I wouldn't have been able to get acquainted with Jenny, the waitress that I have. She is a very nice girl and I have talked to her again tonight," Allen replied.

"That's great Allen. Enjoy your evening. I'll see you at work," I said as I started walking back to my table.

Allen told me to have a good evening as well, so I sat there at my table, eating and watching both he and Jenny get closer by the second. It had brought back a bunch of memories for me, but I knew that with this being the start of a new beginning for me, I felt like I had done the right thing.

The next day, being Sunday, was another day of going back out to the ranch. I could have gone somewhere with my friends, but chose not to. Mike was the president of one of the banks in town and, of course, full of himself. He had done well for himself, but being the fast talker that he was, he might have done what I did when I lived in Newark and made up a bunch of horse crap to get the position that he did at the bank. With everything that I knew, I was glad that I had changed banks before Mike became the president, knowing that some of my money could have ended up in his pocket as I had learned from the best, and he was the biggest liar and player that I knew other than myself.

The day at the ranch was great as I not only got to see Mother and Father, but also Pam. As we sat down at the table for dinner, there were more questions coming from Pam where I was concerned, and also some talk about what Carl was doing now.

"Robbie, have you thought about moving East?" Pam asked.

At that time I almost choked on a bite of food that I had put in my mouth. If Pam only knew that I had gone East and had lived for around 28 years in the huge city of Newark.

"I have given it some thought. I know there is a lot of opportunity in the bigger cities there. For the moment, though, I think I am content to stay where I am. How about you? Where are you going to live next, or are you going to make Bakersfield your home forever?" I asked.

"No, I don't want to live and die there, Robbie. It is an alright city, but someday I hope to maybe live in Florida. There are plenty of opportunities there as well. Have you heard anything from Carl?" Pam asked.

"No, I can't say that I have. He is a hard one to figure out. I have thought about him from time to time, but I don't have his current address, so there is no way to try to find him," I replied.

"I am sure he is probably still driving around the city somewhere, trying to pick up girls," Pam said as she laughed.

I was doing some laughing at what she had said and Father felt the need to tell Pam and me that no matter what Carl was doing at that time, he was our brother, and if we couldn't respect him for anything else, then we had to respect that about him. Then he added, "Please pass the mashed potatoes." At that time, all of us started laughing. I was enjoying my time with my family so much.

After we had all had a good laugh at Carl's expense, we sat around the table, talking about other things and finishing our meal. When I left there, I had gone back to my apartment to relax. As for Allen and Jenny, I had decided to let things take their course as I had set things in motion, and now it was time to see later if history repeated itself, and whether or not Allen would ask Jenny to marry him like I had done.

Months went by with Allen coming to work every day with a big smile on his face and telling me that he was very happy and that he thought that he had found the love of his life. Allen also mentioned that he was going to see if Jenny would become his wife. I told Allen that I was very happy for them both, and that someday I would be uniting with my true love that lived around the Chicago area, when the time was right. I am not sure that Allen believed me, but I didn't care as the weight had been removed from me and I couldn't be happier for them.

Within a few months, Jenny was walking down the aisle to join Allen at the altar, where they said their vows to one another. When the minister asked if anyone objected or had anything to say, I wanted to stand up and say, "Allen, you have no idea what a liar Jenny is. Be careful as she will not respect your wishes and will throw you under a bus the first chance that she gets." Instead, I just sat there and knew that Allen would find out about Jenny soon enough.

I was a free man and extremely happy! I looked at Kelly during the ceremony and she was smiling. I was sure that she would have picked Allen over me from the beginning 31 years ago, and that was just fine!

More time went by, and Allen had come to work with a big smile on his face. He announced to all of us that he was going to be a father and that he couldn't be happier. I once again smiled at him as I knew that I had done the right thing, and that David wasn't going to grow up without a father being there for him. As for Jenny, I didn't know whether she would still pass away years later from a blood disease. This was up to God.

My life had turned a corner and all I could do was sit back and see what was going to happen next.

Nine months had passed and Allen walked through the company front door, carrying cigars for all of us. He said that Jenny had given birth to a baby boy and that his name was David. This was the same day and date 31 years ago that I had left Kingston, going East to find a job in Newark.

I was surprised the next morning, when I opened my eyes and I was still in Kingston. Apparently, my journey there wasn't done. I was expecting to be in Newark and trying to figure out how to undo all of the damage that I had created while I was living there.

All of the money that I basically stole from the companies that I not only worked for, but the ones that I had created, was sitting in my bank in Apple Grove, where I was living before the coin took me back in time.

Since I was still here, there had to be something else that I needed to find out about or learn before I would travel on to a different place. My thoughts were that I needed to visit my old friend Mike again. While growing up, he was a bad influence on me. I guess because I admired him way too much for the way that he was, with me being the shy boy in school and him being popular with the girls, being deceitful, a cheater, liar, and a player with everyone. In my mind I had put him on a pedestal. Mike was someone who knew what he wanted and went after it. I was the follower that didn't know what I wanted at that time of my life. I had to find a way to turn things around, or put him where I was during the time when I had become like him with my thoughts and actions. This would mean somehow getting him to go to Newark, instead of me. In other words, I had to create the right moment like I had done with Allen and Jenny. Somehow, I would find a new twist where Mike was concerned and make him the bad guy that he already was. This could be more difficult than I thought that it would be.

The only thing that I saw going badly with me doing this was that Mike would be the one that met Taylor instead of me. I wanted Taylor to be all mine the rest of my life. I would need to find a way to ride in on a white horse to save her from him and give her the life that she deserved to have. I needed to save her from the horrible death that I felt that I had created because she was coming to Newark to see me that night. I didn't even know if this was possible, but somehow I had to try.

It had been several years since I had hung out with Mike. After we grew up, he had his own crowd that he hung with, and I had pretty much stayed to myself most of the time except when I went to the ranch to see my parents, to help my father with the livestock. It might be interesting to see how Mike was living now and if he was still the deceitful, arrogant, egotistic man that he was as a kid. I had a journey for him to take and I wasn't sure if my plan was going to work.

After I left my apartment, I went to the bank to talk to Mike. I was sure that after all of these years of me not contacting him that he would be suspicious of why I hadn't. When I walked into the bank, Mike came over to me.

"Rob, it's good to see you again! It has been quite some time since our paths crossed," Mike said.

"It's good to see you too, Mike. I have just been busy

with the work that I do and helping my dad at the ranch," I replied.

"What can I help you with today?" Mike asked.

"I came here to see you today because I have something to pass on to you. I know that you have worked at this bank for some time now, but I heard about an opening in Newark, New Jersey, and the first person that I thought about was you. I know that you have some years of business experience and the job pays very well. There are also benefits to this job as well. I'm not sure if you are interested in leaving Kingston and moving to the city, but if you are, you won't be disappointed," I remarked, hoping that Mike took the bait that I had laid out for him.

"Well, Rob, I hadn't given it much thought on moving to a huge city. I have worked here for several years now and the owner of the bank really likes me. He is always telling me what a great job I have done for him. The pay isn't the best, but I have ways to increase it when I need to," Mike said with the same cocky smile on his face that he had when we were younger.

I knew what he was talking about as I had become like him when I was living and working in Newark and was sure that Mike was dipping into the till of someone's account or maybe many. As I had said before, I was just happy that I didn't have my money in this bank. His old ways had stayed with him as he hadn't changed a bit, and it was up to me now to talk him into traveling East and taking the same direction that I had taken. I knew that he had deceit built into him from the very beginning and that I didn't. In order for my plan to happen, I was going to need to do some fast talking again myself.

"I am sure that you have liked this job, Mike. No doubt there has been some perks to it, but just think about all the perks waiting for you in the city of Newark! There is so much more opportunity of getting rich there than here. I think that you are the right man for this job. There is a chance that I will also be moving to Newark, and if you want, we can hang out some," I said.

"Well, Rob, I will give it some thought and get back to you about this. By the way, how do you know about this job?" Mike asked.

"Let's just say that I have inside connections. Think about it and get back to me as this job won't be available much longer," I replied.

"That's interesting, Rob. I will let you know later today or first thing in the morning whether I want to take this important job in Newark," Mike replied.

"This sounds good, Mike. I'll talk with you after a while," I said as I turned around to walk away.

When I reached the front door of the bank, I turned around and saw that Mike's wheels were turning in his head. He still loved money as much as he did when he was younger, and I also knew that he still could play people and con them out of every cent that they had if he desired it. He was standing there in deep thought and I could see it on his face. Now the wait. I wasn't sure how much longer I had before the coin took me in the direction of Newark.

After I left the bank, I went to the ranch to help Father, and then to the house to talk to Mother. I told them at that time that there was a good chance that I would be leaving Kingston soon and moving to Newark, New Jersey. Of course, they wondered why and asked me if I had a job already lined up there. I told them that I knew of several jobs that were needing someone and that with me knowing this, I was sure that I could find a good paying job to give me more money to live on. I also told them that I wouldn't leave town without saying goodbye, and that I would see them again but that I wasn't sure when it would be.

I could see the look on their faces and it was a sad look. They both thought that I would stay in Kingston the rest of their lives, but they said that they wished me the best if I did leave and that we would continue to talk frequently and see each other when we could. This was hard for me to do, but until I could make things right, I wasn't in charge of my life. The coin was.

When I returned to town, I went to the restaurant where I had eaten many times. After I ordered, I saw Mike coming through the front door. He had a beautiful lady with him as he always did. After they were seated, Mike had spotted me. He excused himself and came over to where I was sitting. Now would be the time for me to find out if he was going to be the one working at Russ-A-Thon instead of me, repeating my history, or if I was going to need to go another route to figure it all out with me returning to Newark to go through each motion that I had made there from the very start of living there the first time.

"Rob, I have made a decision," Mike spoke.

"That's good. What did you decide to do?" I asked, waiting with anticipation for his answer.

"I have decided to quit my job at the bank. I spoke with the owner and he told me that I can return there to work again if I ever choose to. I guess I will be leaving in the morning for Newark. I was planning on stopping by your apartment tonight if I didn't see you in town, to find out the name of the company that is looking for help right now. Even if I don't get hired on there, I am sure there are many more companies that will want me to work for them," Mike replied.

"Before you leave in the morning, come to my apartment and I will give you all the information that you will need after you have arrived in Newark. I will be leaving Kingston soon as well, to also go to Newark. After I arrive, I will look you up and then we can hang out at times. Maybe I can help you find more work if it doesn't work out with the company that is hiring now, or a different one that you can get a job with later on," I said.

"I will do that Rob. It will be nice to have a friend living in the same city that I do. Maybe we can become closer friends," Mike spoke.

"Maybe?" I replied.

Mike walked away and my plan was in motion. It looked

like he took the bait. Now if only my history would repeat itself with him, like it had with Allen and Jenny.

The next morning, I was up and waiting for Mike to show up. I had the address and phone number for Russ-A-Thon. This was the first place that I had worked for, and where I did my first con. If I was correct, when Mike arrived there, it would be the first day that I had gone there, lying through my teeth. The only difference between Mike and me was that he actually had work experience in business and I didn't.

Around 9:00 a.m. I heard a knock at my door. I knew who it was. I was expecting him.

"Mike," I said as I answered the door.

"Rob, are you ready for me?" Mike asked.

"Yes, come in," I replied.

"I am packed and ready to go. I can't wait to see what Newark has to offer me," Mike spoke.

"More than you can even imagine, Mike. The name of the company that is hiring is called Russ-A-Thon. The building is located in a rich part of Newark. It is a good company to work for and you will like the owner. They need a CEO to run the company. Your job is to sell their products to different companies and individuals. I am more than sure that you can handle this and the job pays well," I said as I handed him the information.

"This sounds like it is right up my alley, Rob. Thank you for the tip. This company will be the first one that I go to after I get to Newark. Give me a call when you get there and we'll hang out at one of the clubs," Mike replied.

"Will do, Mike. Have a good journey, and I will keep in touch," I said as I closed the door.

With me not knowing for sure whether the coin was going to take me to Newark, I had to sit back and wait.

That night as I laid in bed, Taylor was on my mind. Somehow with or without the coin, I needed to find her again, and save her from Mike. With everything that I had learned about conning and playing people, I had learned from him, and I knew what he was capable of as I had become him for 30 years. Did I regret everything that I did? The answer was NO. I had many choices to make along my journey from the time I was 23 years old until now. In my mind I wanted to believe that most of them were good. If the coin didn't take me to Newark soon next week, I would call Russ-A-Thon to see if Mike had taken my place and landed the job.

Later in the day, I received a call from Allen. He wanted to tell me how much David had grown. He invited me over to the house to see him and eat dinner with them if I wanted to. I stood there, thinking about it for a minute, and then I told Allen that I probably would be leaving Kingston soon and that I had to get some things put in place before I left.

Allen said he was sorry to see me go, but that he wished me well. I told him to enjoy every day with his family and that someday David was going to grow up and be the owner of a big construction company after he had served his time in the military. Allen told me that would be great!

When he asked me why I thought this, I just told him that I believed it would happen. Allen laughed at that moment and told me that no matter what David did, he would be proud of him. This was when I told Allen that I knew he was a much better father than I ever could be. I meant every word of it and still do.

When Allen and I were done talking, I laid down on the couch to take a nap. When I woke up, I was lying in bed at the dingy motel room in Newark, awaiting Mike's arrival. I guess once again the coin needed to keep me in Kingston a little longer before it took me on this journey. I knew I had changed and was the same way I was before I met Jenny. I had learned that Mike was someone not to admire, but to pity. He had a bunch of changing to do himself, and he was about ready to repeat what I had done and someday maybe he would find a gold coin that would take him back in time to redo all the wrong that he had done to himself and to other people.

—10—

REPAIRING INSTEAD OF REPEATING

When I opened the curtain next to the bed, I saw my old pickup truck sitting there waiting for me. The only thing I had on me was what money that I had in my pocket, and of course the gold coin. I knew that I had to find a job, but this time I would just concentrate on construction companies as this was what I had done for years. I would leave the conning to Mike. He was good at it, like I used to be. Meanwhile, I would be there to see if time repeated itself. If it did, Mike would be the one instead of me that would be making wrong choices in life, having regrets later and needing to change everything that he had done. All I knew was that I wasn't Mike any longer.

That day I did get a call from my parents wanting to know how I had been. I told them that I was doing good in Newark. They told me that they wished me well and to call them soon. I told them that I would. When I left Kingston this time, my family knew where I was, and I laid in bed and smiled. I wasn't running from anyone, or anything, and this time I was going to do things the right way in my life.

After I showered and got dressed, I left the motel room to go to the same construction company that I had gone to 30 years ago. I didn't know if I would get the job or not, but this time I was going there without a cocky attitude like I had years ago. Maybe this would help.

When I walked in the office to fill out an application for the job, the same receptionist once again was smiling at me. She was just as interested this time as she was the time before. I finished the application and handed it to her. I was told that it would be given to the boss for review, and if I got the job, then he would call me back. I thanked her and walked out of there. No lying to her on the application about being a foreman for years.

Later that day, I sat on my bed, wondering if Mike had gotten the job as CEO at Russ-A-Thon. I looked at my watch, and if I was right, he had already left the company either smiling or wondering why he had listened to me if the company didn't want to employ him. It was time to make a call.

"Russ-A-Thon. Can I help you?" my old receptionist said.

"Yes, you can. Is there a way that I can speak with Mike Perez?" I asked.

"Mr. Perez has left for the day. He will be here tomorrow if you would like to call back, or I can take a message for him," she replied.

"I will call back, and thank you," I said with a smile on my face. Once again, history had repeated itself.

I knew that if I had gone there to apply for the job again, I would have had to lie again and con my way into it. I was trying hard to undo the bad choices that I had made. This was going to be the only way that I could have peace within myself. Mike had been a bank president for years and he did have the business savvy that it took to do this. Maybe he would not do what I had done, and only time would tell. If he did, he was still the con artist that I had learned from and would be without a job like I was eventually, as it would all catch up with him.

In the morning I would make it a point to either call him or go there to see him. For now, I had to find a cheap diner to eat at. My lifestyle had changed, just like Jenny wanted it to when I stood at her grave.

The next day I decided to go to Russ-A-Thon to see how Mike was doing. When I entered the receptionist's office, she looked at me and said, "Can I help you?"

"Yes, I have come here to talk to Mr. Perez," I spoke.

"I will see if he is available to talk," she said as she picked up her phone to call him. Mike had given the okay for me to come into his office.

When I heard this, I walked straight ahead to enter the room that I had sat in for years, cheating other people and the company.

"Come in, Rob," Mike said.

"It looks like you got the job, Mike. How do you like it so far?" I asked as I looked on his desk. I saw the same papers that Mr. Jones had put in front of me years ago. In my mind I was wondering what Mike would do with them.

"Thanks for the tip, Rob! As you see, I did get the job. I am sure that I am going to be very happy working for this company. The perks are going to be amazing," Mike replied.

"I know they will be, Mike. I can't stay. I just wanted to come here and see for myself if you had gotten hired. You have my phone number. Give me a call anytime. I will be living here too for a while and working construction like I have for many years," I responded.

"I will do it, old friend! Stay in touch!" Mike said.

I told him that I would, and walked out of the office. There was a part of me that was hoping that Mike would not repeat all the conning that I had done, but the other side of me knew that he would. It would be a while before Mr. Jones found out what a snake Mike actually was. Meanwhile, I would keep in touch with him to see what he did next.

When I returned to the motel, I saw that I had gotten a call on the motel phone from the same construction company that I had gone to. I called them back and was told to start work bright and early in the morning.

Months went by and I hadn't talked to Mike. I was sure that by then if he did what I did, he was living in my old penthouse in the best part of Newark. I decided it was time to pay him a visit to see. After I knocked on the door, he did answer and once again everything was the exact way that it had been before.

"Rob, it is good to see you. Come in for a while," Mike said.

"Hello, Mike. I heard that you were living here now. It looks like you are doing well for yourself," I commented as I entered.

"Yes, I am Rob. You were right, there are many perks working for that company. More than I ever could have imagined," Mike replied.

"I'm sure there are. How do you like Newark now?" I asked.

"I love living here. My receptionist smiles at me a lot and I have met many businessmen since I started working at Russ-A-Thon. Mr. Jones trusts me and pretty much leaves me alone to do what I want to do. Did you ever find a job?" Mike asked.

"Yes, I am working. My job doesn't pay as well as yours does, but it is good honest work," I said

"That's good, Rob. I hate to chase you off as you just got here, but I am on my way to a club in hopes of bringing back a couple of women to keep me company," Mike responded.

"I understand, Mike. I have been there before, so I know what you mean. Call me and let me know how your life turns out," I said with a smile as I already knew the ending to his story at Russ-A-Thon.

"I will, and you keep in touch as well," Mike replied.

I had walked to the door by then. I told Mike goodbye and walked away. It was very clear that Mike was making the same mistakes with his choices as I had when I, too, worked as CEO in the exact chair that he was now sitting in at Russ-A-Thon. It wouldn't be long until Mr. Jones would be firing him and, at this time it would be interesting to see if his life took him in the same direction that mine had taken me.

I had left the penthouse and everything looked like it

was when it belonged to me years ago. Mike's journey that he was taking at that moment was the same one that I was on when I lived in Newark and worked for Russ-A-Thon.

More months had passed and by then I had found a cute small apartment that was big enough for maybe two or three people. I had money in the bank and wasn't doing too badly for myself. Instead of hundreds of dollars that I had sitting in my bank, I knew that Mike had thousands sitting in his.

That day while I was out on a job, I had ended up at the house of Sam Heatherton. He was the owner of Heatherton Incorporated, where I had worked during the time when I met Taylor. Mr. Heatherton didn't recognize me and I was fairly sure that he wouldn't. The job opening for CEO at his company hadn't come up yet. If once again my journey continued to become Mike's journey, and with him living the same life that I had led him to, Mike would be the man that Mr. Heatherton would hire to be the new CEO.

This would only happen this way if the gold coin that I had carried in my pocket for many years wanted it to be that way. If not, it would have a different idea that I would foresee later on. I wanted to believe that the coin had sent me to Mr. Heatherton that day to work on his home.

The sad part was that I did like Sam Heatherton and Ted Jones. Many people, including their companies, had taken a beating because of me from the con artist act that I had inherited from Mike, admiring him for everything he said and did when we were in school. I wasn't sure that I could make things right with all the people that I had hurt. I knew that most of them I would never see again.

As I was working on Mr. Heatherton's home, he stopped me so that we could talk.

"Robert, you are doing an amazing job. I couldn't be happier with your work. I wish I had a guy like you working for me at my company, Heatherton Industries. If you ever decide to change professions and quit the construction business, I would very much like it if you would give me a call and I will find room in my company for you doing something. Good workers are hard to find nowadays."

This was what I needed to hear. I could go back to Heatherton Industries and, even though I wouldn't be the CEO there, I could still work hard for Mr. Heatherton and earn my paycheck the right way, like everyone else did there.

At that moment I told him that there was a good chance that I would be calling him, and I thanked him for thinking of me and wanting me to work for his company. I also told him that I was a hard worker and would give it everything that I had as I was also a fast learner and could learn any job where he wanted to place me.

Mr. Heatherton told me to call him anytime I was ready to, and that I would have a job waiting for me. I thanked him and told him that at that time I needed to leave as I had another construction job that I needed to go to before the end of the day. My job at Mr. Heatherton's house had been completed.

When I met Taylor, I was working for Heatherton Incorporated, and now I had to figure out how I was going to meet Steve, Taylor's uncle, so that I could get an invitation to the big dinner party that I knew they would be having at their home. I had to be there to intercept what could go badly with Mike being there at the same time and being the tour guide to take Taylor to different scenic spots around Newark instead of me. Steve and Nikki's dinner party was where I had first laid eyes on Taylor. I wanted it perfect, just like it was many years ago. I was going to give it everything that I had to win Taylor's love away from Mike, if he showed up that night for the party.

At the end of the day of work, I went back to my apartment. I had a lot of planning to do. While I was sitting on my couch, thinking, I got a call from Mike.

"Hello, Mike," I said.

"Hello, Rob. I have some news for you that you might be interested in," he said.

"What would that be, Mike?" I asked.

"I just wanted to let you know that I'm not employed

with Russ-A-Thon any longer. I quit the job. My receptionist was getting a little too close to me, and I didn't want to mix business with pleasure in my work place. So, I told Mr. Jones that I couldn't work for him any longer and walked out of my office," Mike spoke.

"*Wow*, Mike! That had to be hard for you to do," I said as in my thoughts I knew that Mike was a huge liar. Because of what had happened to me when I worked for them, doing what I did to Mr. Jones and his company, I was sure that Mike had gotten himself in a mess, with his true colors finally showing. I knew he had gotten fired!

"Would you like to eat out at a fancy restaurant with me tonight, Rob?" Mike asked.

"Yes, that sounds great, Mike. I know of a very nice place in the Bronx called Merci. It is a French restaurant that has a wonderful selection of cuisine," I replied.

I could hear by Mike's voice that he was shocked that I would even know about a restaurant this nice, and he even asked me how I knew about it. My words back to him were, "Mike, I have connections for many different things."

I got dressed up in the nicest suit that I had and went to meet him, to enjoy a very expensive meal, and of course my iced tea.

When I was escorted to my seat where Mike was waving the waiter over, it was like many years ago, when I had gone there to eat several times. After I sat down and the waiter left, Mike and I started talking.

"I'm happy you could join me tonight, Rob. It's been fun seeing you since both of us have moved here," Mike said.

"Me too, Mike! This place is one of the most elegant restaurants in Newark. Only the rich eat here. On my salary right now, I am happy that you are going to be the one that pays for our meal," I said as I laughed.

"Don't worry, Rob. I have you covered tonight. I made quite a bit of money working for Russ-A-Thon. The perks were even better," Mike replied with a smile.

"So now what's next, Mike? Are you going to keep your

penthouse and stay here, or are you going back to Kingston to your old job?" I asked.

"I'm staying here in Newark for now, Rob. I have a lead on something else that I want to do. I believe that it is going to make me more money," Mike replied.

"What's that, Mike?" I asked.

"I have been pretty good at betting on the right horses at the track, and I think that is what I am going to do for now. I will get another job when I see that a good company is hiring. Right now, I need a break and some entertainment," Mike spoke.

"That sounds interesting, Mike. I know of someone that did very good at the tracks," I spoke, not telling him that person that I was referring to was myself years ago.

"We'll see, Rob, as I will move on to something else after a while. Newark is my home for now, thanks to you," Mike responded.

"I'm glad that you like the city," I replied, looking at Mike, but thinking that the only thing that he really liked about it was all the stolen money that he had sitting in his bank account, just like I did back then when I was him. If he could pull off the cons that he was doing in Kingston, he would have still been there. He knew that there were more trusting people in Newark, waiting to be taken for a ride, than there were in our country town where we had grown up.

Mike and I sat and ate. After we had finished eating, I thanked him for the dinner and an evening out in the city. I then told him that I had to leave as it was going to be another early morning of work for me in the morning

At that time, Mike said that he, too, had to leave as he was going to a club for some different kind of entertainment. Of course, I knew again what he was talking about. I had been there.

While driving to my apartment, I was once again thinking about Taylor. She had been on my mind since the first day that I laid eyes on her. I had come up with a plan, not knowing whether it would work or not, but because I desperately wanted to spend my life with the only woman that I knew that I could truly love. I had decided that it was time for me to be back in Steve and Nikki's life. I wanted to make sure that I would get an invitation to their party that I was sure they would have if time repeated itself with them as well.

The longer that I waited, the more difficult it was going to be. Tomorrow afternoon, when I was done with work, I was going to their home to give Steve one of my business cards from the company that I was currently working for.

If things worked out well, I would get invited into their home to sit down with Steve and Nikki and talk to them about what work I have done in their neighborhood. Maybe, if they were interested, they would want me to do some work for them, and this could be the beginning of hopefully a friendship with them. With us being friends long before the date of the dinner party, and the first time that I had met Taylor, it might be what I needed to keep Taylor from hooking up with Mike, and instead falling in love with me once more.

For now, all I wanted to think about was getting some sleep. I had a busy week at work, and more work scheduled for me tomorrow around Newark. I knew that Steve liked to talk, so if nothing else, maybe we could become friends with us having talking parties, or even tea parties. Now I was being silly. I had to laugh at myself.

My day at work the next day went quicker than I thought it would. When I had completed each job that I was sent out on, I went home to shower and change clothes. Then, I got in my truck and drove to Steve and Nikki's mansion. Once again, I looked around at all of the expensive cars that were parked at different homes around the area and laughed again as my old truck might stink up the neighborhood.

I parked, and walked to the front door, not knowing what to expect. This was going to be interesting, and if I got turned away at the door, then I would find a different way to meet and talk to Steve, even if it meant going to the company where he worked.

To my surprise, when I rang the doorbell, Steve was the one who answered the door.

"Hello, can I help you?" Steve asked.

"Yes. I have done several home improvement jobs in and around your neighborhood and the entire area of Newark, and I was wondering if you would be interested in our services someday. I have a card to give you from the company where I am employed, if you would like one," I spoke.

"Well, son, why don't you come into the house and we can talk about this? By the way, I love your old truck! I have several old vehicles sitting in my garage that I have restored. I have entered them in many competitions and they are my show pieces. I am very proud of them. When we finish with our conversation, if you don't mind, I would like to take a look at your beauty that you are driving," Steve commented.

"No, I wouldn't mind a bit," I said as I walked with Steve into his house.

"I didn't ask you your name," Steve said.

"My name is Robert Stone," I spoke.

"I'm Steve Andrews. You can call me Steve if you like. I haven't ever liked being referred to as Mr. Andrews as it sounds so formal.

"Okay, Steve it is," I commented.

"Would you like something to drink, Robert?" Steve asked.

"Yes, I would. It has been a hot day today. Iced tea would work good for me, Steve. I don't drink alcohol," I said.

"Iced tea it is, coming right up," Steve commented as he walked away from me to a mini bar that was sitting in the living room. He opened the door and pulled out a pitcher of tea from the small refrigerator. My guess was that maybe Nikki also liked tea.

"So, tell me Robert, what kind of construction are you doing?" Steve asked.

"I work for a company called Roberts Incorporated. We

build homes and also remodel them. This is what I have been doing for many years now. I come from a small town called Kingston, Utah. I grew up there and decided to stick around there for a while. Then, years ago, I thought about coming here to Newark and have been here ever since," I replied.

"*Wow!* It sounds like you have been a very busy young man. I remember having your kind of energy when I was much younger. I do have some things that I would like to remodel in here, and soon I will give your company a call and ask for you to be the one that they send out on the job. Before then, though, if you are in the neighborhood, stop by and we can visit from time to time. I like you. You seem to be an honest, polite, young man. I have a niece that I think that you would hit it off with. One of these days, she told me that she will be visiting my wife, Nikki and me. At that time, I will give you a call so that you can meet her. She is around your age and is a very nice girl," Steve said.

"I would really like that, Steve! I have no one in my life as I am a single guy. Next week I will be back sometime, even if I don't have a job in the neighborhood. We can sit and talk, if you like. I don't have very many friends yet here in Newark," I responded.

"That would be great, Robert. I am looking forward to seeing you again soon. Meanwhile, let's go outside and take a look at your prize possession that you have sitting in the driveway," Steve said.

We walked out the door and to the truck, where Steve was amazed at how nice it was. I had taken good care of it since I bought it. He told me that if I ever wanted to sell it that he was interested in buying it and would give me top dollars for it. I told him that I would consider his offer, and that I would be back in a few days to see him and to meet his wife.

Steve was very happy about that. I, at that moment, got the impression that Steve was kind of a lonely man inside with maybe not very many friends, who just wanted to sit, and talk with me. Maybe this is why he kept wanting me to come in the house years ago after I had brought Taylor home—to sit, talk and drink that glass of iced tea. Now I would know Steve on a different level, and so far I liked this one much better.

After I left Steve and Nikki's home, I headed back to my apartment. I knew that trip to talk to Steve was worth it. I needed to get my foot in the door, which I had. When it was the right date of the time when Taylor first flew to Newark to visit for a few weeks, I would get to see my beautiful Taylor once again. The rest of the drive home, all I could do was smile.

That night, I had decided to get dressed up and go to a nicer restaurant than where I had been eating at in the better part of the city. I had gotten a small bonus from the company that I worked for and was going to treat myself to a good meal.

When I was seated, I saw Mike coming through the front door. Of course, I waved to the waiter to let him know that I would like to have Mike at my table. He was alone, but I knew before the end of the night that he would be looking for any woman that would give him a smile, and maybe more than that. During the time when I had turned into Mike, I had a huge ego, and thought that I, too, was God's gift to any woman. I had learned from the best, and at that time it was Mike.

"Rob, it is good to see you in here. I didn't think that with the job that you have you could afford a place this nice to eat out in," Mike said with once again a cocky smile.

"My company gave me a bonus, and I decided to do something nice for myself. I didn't expect to run into you here tonight," I replied.

"There are times when I do come in here. It isn't the nicest place to eat in Newark, but they do have really good food," Mike responded.

"I have also been here before during the time that I have lived here. I agree with the food being fantastic," I commented.

"What have you been doing lately? Are you still betting on the horses?" I asked.

"No. I got bored with that, Rob. I was winning every time that I went to the track, but I wanted to do something else with my time in between jobs. I went to a boxing match the other night downtown. I saw a couple of young boxers that I really liked. They are young, but can really fight. They knew just when to knock out their opponent. I happened to run into their trainers, and after we had talked for a while about the young boxers, I decided to put some money into them and finance what they needed. So now it is the waiting game, to see if I made a good investment and choice doing this with them," Mike replied.

"That sounds interesting, Mike. I am sure that the two that you picked will be a great investment. One of these nights, maybe I will join you to watch them box," I said.

"That would be great, Rob. If you do, we can make it a night of fun and maybe go to a little nicer place to eat than this one is. Besides work, what have you been doing?" Mike asked.

"Not much, Mike, but I did make a new friend today. He is a business man like you, and we seemed to hit it off," I spoke.

"Maybe *I* will get to meet him someday as well," Mike replied.

"I'm sure that you will. It shouldn't be much longer before you do," I spoke.

Once again, Mike looked at me kind of funny. I think he thought that I had a crystal ball in my back pocket, telling me everything that was about to happen in the world. We changed subjects and sat there, eating and enjoying the fact that we weren't eating alone, or should I say that *I* wasn't.

After I left there and went back to my apartment, once again I was thinking about Taylor. I knew that it was going to be a while before the date of her arrival, and between now and then I was going to get as close to Steve and Nikki as I could. They would want to know what made me tick, and I wanted to show them the honest guy that they needed to get to know, and not the egotistical, arrogant, cheating, lying, self-centered Robert, the con artist, that they had met before and had no idea about.

Back then, if Taylor wouldn't have died in the plane crash, I wanted to believe that I would have changed as I really did love her, but with my con jobs that I did, and the conning that I kept doing even after meeting and falling in love with her, I felt like eventually she would have found out about everything. If she did, I wouldn't have had her by my side until the day that I died. This time, she was going to meet the *real* Robert Stone and not a fake replica of Mike.

That week after I got off from work, I went back home to shower and change clothes. I had decided to go visit with Steve for a while. Of course, when I got there, he was very happy to see me. We sat and talked for a couple of hours about many things.

Steve told me that he had grown up with many brothers and sisters. He said that his mother and father were very poor and that it was hard for them to make ends meet sometimes. When he was younger, he had gotten mixed up with a bad crowd that took him down a dark path for a while, until he realized that he had to choose a different direction for his life. He said that he had made several choices that he wished that he could go back and change.

There were parts of his story that reminded me of some of my own. Steve said that when he met Nikki, he was working for a meat-packing plant. She came from a fairly well-to-do family, and he said that when he looked at her, it was love at first sight. They were two different people and he wasn't sure that they could make a marriage work, but because they wanted to be together, no matter what happened, they got married. He said that they had been married for 40 years. He also told me that they couldn't have any children of their own, but had many nieces and nephews that they loved to spoil. I was learning a lot about Steve.

At that time I knew that he wasn't the rich snob that

I thought he was when I had met him the first time, many years ago.

When Steve had finished telling me his life story for the day, I felt at that moment like the gold coin in my pocket was one of the best things that had happened to me. It gave me the opportunity to go back in time and redo the bad parts of my past. For this, I would be forever grateful.

Our visits over the next several months became more frequent, and Steve and I had become best friends. We had gone to several places together, and I had become very close to Nikki as well. It was as if we were already one big happy family, and I hadn't met Taylor yet.

As for Mike, he had still continued on with the same journey that I took and was in the stock broker business that he created, like I had, conning many people, right and left out of thousands of dollars, and not caring who he hurt in the process. I knew that eventually he would decide to get out while he could, like I had done. It wouldn't be much longer and he would be working for Sam Heatherton, the owner of Heatherton Industries.

At the time when Sam offered me a job in his company, not long after I had returned to Newark for the second time, I thought that eventually I would end up there again, working in a different spot for his company. Now I wasn't sure that I wanted to go back there to work. It would be hard for me to be there, watching Mike each day cheating and stealing money from Sam and from Heatherton Industries.

For now, I had decided to stay at my construction job as it paid well and it also gave out a quarterly bonus to all the employees each year. If I did return to Heatherton Industries, it would be after Mike had stopped working there and left the city, going back to Kingston, or to a different job that I knew nothing about at this time.

There was a part of me that was homesick to see my family, but until it was the right time to leave Newark, I would be here working whenever I could and waiting for Taylor to come back into my life once again.

I had decided to sell Steve my old truck. It had done me well for many years, but I felt like it was time to let it go to Steve, who I knew would take really good care of it. It was a classic antique and worth a lot of money. Steve loved the truck, and so he wrote me out a check for $300,000. This was way more money than I expected. I tried to tell him that he didn't need to give me that much money for it, but he insisted saying that the truck now was going to be his prize possession and would have the lead spot in his garage. He said that he would be entering it in many competitions. I signed the title over to him and now it would be his beauty forever.

That day Steve took me to several dealerships to look for a new vehicle. It was time for me to get a car this time. I was no longer a kid cruising up and down main street in the small town of Kingston with a bunch of friends riding in the back of my pickup truck. Instead, I saw a beautiful light blue Porsche. It would be a dream to ride in, and someday soon, I would have Taylor by my side in that car, traveling to many places with me.

With the money that was left from the sale of my truck, and what I had managed to save from my job for many years, I had in my bank account $850,000. I had learned that hard work and honesty would make anyone richer than they started out to be, and that nothing good ever came out of stealing from any place or anyone.

After Steve told me goodbye, I called up Mike. I asked him to join me at a fancy restaurant. I would not only be the one to pick up the check this time, but to show him that I was doing fairly well myself in Newark. Also, I needed to know what he was doing at that time.

"Rob, this is a surprise," Mike said as he sat down at the table.

"Hello, Mike. It has been quite a while since I have seen you. I wanted to treat you tonight with a good dinner like you did me one time. This is my way of paying you back. How is everything going with you?" I replied.

"I am doing good. I am working now for a company called Heatherton Incorporated. The perks at this job are just as good, if not better, than they were when I worked for Russ-A-Thon. I gave up the broker business," Mike responded.

"I have been to that building before, and it is a nice company. The fashions that they put out are very expensive and beautiful. The models aren't bad to look at either," I spoke as I once again looked at Mike's face. He looked like a deer caught between two headlights, wondering how a man on my salary would see the inside of that company and also the models as they were only at the company when a fashion show was happening. Only rich people with invitations were allowed in to watch. So, he sat there with a confused look on his face.

"Yes, they are beautiful for sure, Rob," Mike said, still looking confused.

"How is Sam doing?" I asked with a cocky smile, trying to let Mike see what he looked like when he smiled like that.

"He's good," Mike replied, still wondering how I knew Mr. Heatherton's first name.

By then I decided to give Mike a break, so I changed the subject.

"My new friend that I was telling you about bought my old truck. He really liked it and wanted to add it to his collections. We have become pretty close since I last saw you," I said.

"What did he give you for the truck?" Mike asked.

"Enough to buy a new Porsche," I replied.

"*Wow,* I didn't think that old truck was worth that much. He paid you well for it. A new Porsche is not cheap," Mike responded.

By then the waiter had brought our food and we sat there and talked about other things. Mike told me that his receptionist wasn't as young as the last one was, but that she was very efficient. I told Mike that I was sure that she had a kind heart as well. I asked if he had made some big bucks working at the broker business. He told me that he had, but then he decided to make up the excuse that he had to quit it because he was getting too many clients wanting to invest with him, and that he had no time for himself. Of course, I knew that he was lying to me. The reason why he gave it up was the same reason why I had. The truth was that he was nervous about getting caught.

After we ate and had caught up on our lives after we last saw each other, Mike thanked me for dinner and said that he would call me soon, and we could maybe go eat at a different fancy restaurant sometime, and that it would be on him next time to pick up the check. He also mentioned us going to a club for some real entertainment. I told him that would be nice and that I would see him another time before too long. Mike left and I went home. I could have cared less about going clubbing with him.

The next morning, before I went to work, it dawned on me that this coming Saturday would be the date that Taylor and I would meet in three weeks. When I went to Steve and Nikki's home this weekend, more than likely Steve would be telling me that Taylor was coming to visit them. Hopefully at that time I would get an invitation to the dinner party. I had done some serious thinking about Mike and I had a different plan that I wanted to put into motion.

I knew that Mike had already met Steve at Russ-A-Thon. When I told Mike that I had made a new friend that was a businessman, I didn't tell him the name of the person I was speaking about. I also remembered the night and date that Steve saw me in the restaurant. This was the night that I got my invitation to the dinner party.

As it got closer to the time of Taylor's arrival, I would follow through with my plan for Mike. Knowing him the way that I did, I was fairly sure that it would work. I just hoped that the coin and I were both in agreement with what I wanted to do.

Once again, the rest of the week went by fast and it was Saturday. I was excited and was planning on spending more time with Steve and Nikki today, unless they had plans of their own.

After I had rang the doorbell, Nikki answered the door.

"Come in, Robert!" Nikki said.

"Thank you, Nikki. Is Steve here?" I asked.

"Steve is outside in the back yard, paying our paperboy. He should be back in the house soon. Please sit down. Would you like some tea?" Nikki asked as she went to the mini bar to pour me a glass.

"That would be great. It is another warm day today," I replied.

"Just to let you know, Robert, Steve really enjoys your company. He loves it when you come over to visit. He has had a bunch of fun as well when you two have gone places together. Thank you for being such a good friend," Nikki spoke.

"I have really enjoyed visiting with both of you. Steve is a great friend of mine and the nicest man that I have ever met, It has been a pleasure getting to know both of you, Nikki. Steve and I have become very close friends over the past several months, and I wish that I could have gotten to know him when I first arrived in Newark," I commented.

"I know that Steve feels the same way about you! As you probably already know, Steve doesn't have very many close friends. When you came into his life, it was a blessing," Nikki responded.

As Nikki had finished her words to me, Steve walked into the room. He was once again very happy to see me.

"Robert, my boy, I am so happy that you came over today. I was hoping that you would find the time to," Steve spoke.

"Steve, there is no other place today that I would rather be. I don't know of anyone that I would rather be around than you two," I said.

"Robert, we feel the same way about you. In fact, we are having a dinner party in a few weeks. We both would love it if you could make it. Our niece is flying in from Chicago to visit. I would really like to introduce her to you. I spoke about her to you once before, and I think that you two will really hit it off. She is around your age," Steve spoke.

Steve, Nikki and I sat there talking for hours that day. We were learning a lot about each other. It felt good to be honest with them. I had told them about my family and also about how shy I was growing up and in school. I even told them about Pam and Carl. I had shared with them information that I didn't think that I would share with anyone in Newark. Mike was the only one living there that knew about me, my family and my life.

Nikki told me about her rich family and where she had grown up. She also shared with me about where she and Steve had met and fallen in love. She told me that she had grown up in a mansion on a hill, where the nanny was the one who took care of her and her sisters. Nikki said that there were many times when she envied her friends because they always had a close relationship with their parents, unlike the one that she had with hers. She even mentioned to me that she wished in her life that she could go back in time to pick new parents for herself, if it was possible.

She loved her parents, but didn't love the fact that because they were so rich, they were too busy with their careers and had the nanny take care of her and her sisters every day while they were either working or off on a trip of some sort. When she met Steve, she said—like me—Steve had told her that it was love at first sight. Also, that what attracted her to him was the fact that he was a poor man who came from a poor family.

Her parents wanted her to marry a rich man, like her sisters did, but she said that each one of her sisters had been divorced more than once, and she always believed that it was because they chose to marry for money and not for love. Nikki said that she and Steve had worked hard for what they had, with no help from her parents.

Because of both of them doing this, they appreciated it more than either one of them would have if they had taken the money from them. Her parents wanted to give money to them so that they wouldn't be struggling until they could make more money of their own, and Nikki had told her parents NO! She also felt like their life together was complete, even if they were childless. She said that their love for each other was worth more to them than anything that they could ever buy, or had.

This was a much different Nikki than I had met the first time years ago. Before, when I met her the night of the dinner party, Nikki hardly spoke to me or any of the other guests. I suppose this was another reason why I got the impression that they were just two rich people that were nothing but snobs, not knowing the truth about how their life started out to be. The one that was the actual snob was *me* for not taking the time to really get to know them.

As for Steve, he sat there and let Nikki talk. I could see that he was deeply in love with her, just like I was with Taylor. That night I learned that a person can't always judge another person by a first impression. Sometimes that is deceiving, and I was grateful to have the opportunity to get to know the real Nikki and Steve. If It hadn't been for this coin taking me back in time, I would have continued on with my life, not just making more bad choices to live with the rest of my life, but also not knowing that they were different people than I believed them to be.

The night that I had called Steve and Nikki to tell them that Taylor's plane had crashed, and he told me that it was my fault, and that I should have been the one that died, was just his emotions talking. He was heartbroken just like I was. Both Nikki and Steve loved Taylor like a daughter. Now I understood why he used the words that he had toward me. After I had talked to him and he said what he had to me, instead of curling up in a ball and feeling sorry for just myself, I should have been a man and returned to their house to talk to both of them.

At that time, once again I was thinking about no one but myself. When I became more bitter after that, it was because of continually making bad choices for myself and blaming everyone again for not just the bad life that I chose for myself, but also for not recognizing that night and for years afterward, that knowing that Steve and Nikki were enduring real pain, and it was nothing that they deserved.

I stayed at their home for many hours and all three of us had bonded even more. I chose not to ask them questions about Taylor as I already knew her story. She had told me about her life, and at the time I believed that she was being honest with me about everything, including her feelings for me.

Nikki and Steve invited me to stay and eat with them, and we talked some more. Around 9:00 p.m., I told them that it had been a long day for all of us and that I was very thankful to know both of them. I also told Steve that I was looking forward to meeting their niece and that I knew that she would be a wonderful lady, just like her Aunt Nikki.

Of course, Nikki smiled and thanked me for my kind words. I told her that I meant everything that I had said. After we stood up from the couch, they followed me to the door to tell me good night and to come back soon. I told them that I would. It was like having family living in Newark, and I was loving it.

—11—

ANTICIPATING AND WAITING

As the days went by, my anticipation of knowing that soon I would get to see Taylor again, and be able to hold her in my arms once again, was becoming even stronger. I had waited many years to be able to do this again. She was the only thing that I could think about.

The next few weeks went by slowly. The week of Taylor's arrival, after I made sure that Steve had seen Mike in the restaurant, and had invited him to the party, I would be putting my plan into motion regarding Mike.

I had been to Steve and Nikki's home many times. The last time that I went, I found out something about Taylor that she had forgotten to mention to me. I knew the reason why. Taylor had also grown up in a rich family. Her mother was Nikki's sister. I was pretty sure that the reason why this subject didn't come up was because Taylor saw that I had money to burn.

Nikki told me that Taylor didn't turn out spoiled like her sisters and brothers did. She said that all Taylor ever wanted out of life was to be able to find a good, honest, caring, loving man, unlike her husband, Albert, whom she had divorced years ago. With this information, it told me that Taylor was a lot like her Aunt Nikki, and that the first time that she fell in love with me with all of the attention that I gave her, that somehow she could see my heart, and this was why she loved me. She didn't care about the size of my wallet. With my now knowing this information about her, it gave me the encouragement of knowing that Taylor would once again learn to love me regardless of the fancy job that I had or my bank account. Once again I felt confident and had to smile.

Finally, the last few weeks slowly came and went. It was the week of Taylor's arrival and Friday night being the same day that I had met Steve in the restaurant, when I had gotten the invitation to the dinner party. Now was the time to move my plan forward and play my winning hand that I held when I saw Mike.

That night I went to the same restaurant where I had seen Steve years ago. I saw Mike sitting at the same table that I had sat at. I knew that within a matter of seconds, Steve would walk through the door and spot Mike. He then would go over to him to talk. I couldn't change this course of events happening, but I might be able to change the outcome. I could only try.

I had picked a table in a darker part of the restaurant, where I could see both Mike and Steve. I looked at my watch and was sure that the next person that would be entering the restaurant would be Steve. History had repeated itself again, and Steve saw Mike and was walking over to Mike's table to talk to him. They would more than likely have the same conversation that Steve and I had years ago.

Everything was looking like it had before. Steve shook Mike's hand and they began talking. After a while, Steve walked away to another table and Mike continued to sit at his and eat. I was wondering if I should take a chance and walk over to Mike's table to talk to him, but I knew that if I did, Steve would see me and come over there. I chose to stay where I was, drinking my iced tea and watching. I wanted to talk to Mike when he was all alone, and after Steve had left.

After a period of watching Steve sit at a table where he had ordered some takeout food, I saw him pay the check and leave the restaurant. Now was my time that I had been waiting for.

"Mike," I said.

"Oh, hello, Rob. I am surprised to see you here tonight," Mike replied.

"I had a hunch that you might be here and I haven't spoken with you for a while, so I thought that I would come here to eat, in hopes of seeing you here," I said.

"Well, your hunch was right, Rob. I have been in here for a while. Not long after I arrived, a man that I had met when I worked for Russ-A-Thon, spotted me and came over to talk to me," Mike commented.

"Oh, what did he want? Did he offer you a job?" I asked, knowing darn full and well that he hadn't.

"No. It appears that he and his wife are throwing a dinner party tomorrow night. He came over here to invite me to it. I guess his niece that lives in Chicago is flying in tomorrow and will also be there. He asked me if I would attend his shindig," Mike replied.

"Are you going?" I asked.

"I told him that I would consider going, but I am wondering if he only wants me to go to his party so that he and his wife can try to play matchmaker and hook me up with his niece. This girl must really look like a dog for her uncle to be drumming up dates for her by asking single men to go there to meet her. I am not sure I am interested in that. You have seen the kind of women that I hang out with since we were in school," Mike responded.

"Oh, I know, Mike. Only the prettiest and best," I said, knowing that Taylor would be the prettiest girl that Mike had ever seen.

"I think that this dinner party can go on without me, and that I am going to pass on going to it. I can go to the club and get more entertainment than I can get at his home. Plus, instead of one girl, I can have two on each arm if I choose to," Mike said.

"This might be a good idea, Mike. I am sure that there

will be someone there at his party that she will hook up with before the night has ended. If you change your mind, let me know," I spoke.

I could see the confusion on Mike's face once more. He was wondering why he would need to let me know anything about his personal life and what he was doing.

"Okay, I can do that," he spoke at that time, not wanting to tell me that what he did was his business.

By then he had finished eating and he told me to have a good night. He left. This plan was different than the one that I had concocted, but in spite of this, it was going to work just as well. I was wondering if the gold coin in my pocket had anything to do with this, or if it, too, was wondering what had just happened as maybe its plan was different as well. All I knew was that by the time that Mike met Taylor, if he did, she would already be taken by me.

After my talk with Mike, I went home to try to sleep. Once again out of excitement of being able to see Taylor the next day, I found myself tossing and turning most of the night. I wanted to look my best for the dinner party and I did have a nice suit with nice shoes to match. Everything I owned wasn't as expensive as it was years ago when I attended the dinner party, but I was sure that it was presentable enough this time around.

Finally, after going over many things in my mind, I drifted off to sleep.

The next day, when the sun shone through my bedroom window, I was wide awake. Today was the day that I had been waiting for. My excitement was soaring! I kept thinking about what Mike had said last night and wondering if he would change his mind and decide to go to the dinner party anyway, just to see if Taylor was the dog that he had said that she probably was. I knew that Taylor was beautiful, and I was hoping that Mike continued to go to the club like he had indicated that he would be doing.

I drank plenty of coffee and was home, waiting until it was time to get ready to go. Many hours passed as I sat on my couch, waiting patiently and wondering if this time around everything would be the same for Taylor and me as it had been years ago.

Finally, it was time for me to leave. I knew that I would be there early once again, so that I would have the time that I needed to talk to Taylor like I had before. The day seemed to pass by quicker than I thought it would, and I was on my way to Steve and Nikki's home. I wanted Taylor to see how close I was to Nikki and Steve. I was nervous and excited at the same time.

After I drove up to the house, there was once again a valet there to take the car to park it. When I rang the doorbell, the same man that answered years ago was checking my name, to see if I was on the guest list. At that time, Steve noticed me at the door and came to assure the man that I was invited. My shoes were shined, my hair was cut, I looked nice, and I was wearing a huge smile.

I could see the back of Taylor as we got closer to her and Nikki. She was wearing the same elegant gown that she had on many years ago. After Steve and I walked over to both Nikki and Taylor, he introduced me to Taylor. It was a repeat of everything, and I was so much in love.

"Taylor, this is my good friend, Robert. He is the man that I told you about," Steve spoke.

"I am pleased to meet you, Robert," Taylor said.

"I am very pleased to meet you as well, Taylor. Your aunt and uncle have told me how happy they are that you came to visit them for a few weeks," I replied.

"I have been looking forward to this visit for some time now. Uncle Steve told me how close you are to him and Aunt Nikki. They told me that you are like family to them," Taylor spoke.

"Yes, your Uncle Steve is my best friend. I am hoping to get to know you while you are here. If you need a tour guide of the tourist sights and the city, I am your man and would be happy to do this," I replied.

"Thank you, Robert. I would love it if you could show

me around the city. Let me know when you want to do this," Taylor commented.

"I work for a construction company that builds homes and remodels them. The best time for me to do this is on the weekend. I am off work at that time. I am also free after work on weekdays. Would you like to go out to eat tomorrow night? At that time we can make plans on where you would like to go and what you would like to see," I responded.

"Yes, that would be very nice. What time should I expect you to be here?" Taylor asked.

"I will pick you up at 5:00 p.m., if this works for you," I said.

"That would be the perfect time for me. Thank you for inviting me to dinner," Taylor said.

"It's my pleasure, Taylor. I hope to make your time here in Newark an enjoyable one," I spoke.

At that time Taylor smiled at me and thanked me again. I didn't waste any time asking her out. I couldn't wait to spend alone time with her. After we had finished our conversation, the doorbell rang and more guests arrived. The same people were here that came to the dinner party years ago. This time I did mingle with them, but it wasn't to find a way to use them later. Taylor continued to look over at me and smile as I did her. There was no sign of Mike.

The night progressed and it wasn't long and the maid had come in to announce that we needed to sit down for dinner at the table. Everything looked the same as before and Taylor was sitting next to me. I wanted to reach over and hug and kiss her and never let go of her, but it was too soon. I had to let her fall in love with me first. This was what happened years ago. This time there was no doubt in my mind, thinking that I didn't need another woman to hang all over me. I couldn't wait until Taylor did. My life had changed and I was on the right track this time.

After the guests left, I sat down on the couch with Steve while we talked, and I drank my glass of iced tea. Taylor and Nikki were talking as well about her flight here. This time

I wanted to stay instead of run. I had nothing to run from. Steve was my best friend as Taylor would be when we were together once again as a couple.

It was getting late and I needed to leave. I told Taylor that I would see her at 5:00 p.m. and shook Steve's and Nikki's hands. I told them that I had a wonderful time and that tomorrow I would be back to not just pick up Taylor, but also to see both of them. They told me that they were excited to see me there again. I left, smiling. My smile wasn't fake and I was very happy. I was on my way home and this night I felt like I would be able to sleep.

In the morning around 9:00, I had a knock at my door. I looked out the peep hole to see who was paying me a visit that early on a Sunday morning. It was Mike.

"Come in, Mike," I said when I opened the door.

"Sorry to come here so early, Rob. I was around the neighborhood and thought that you might be up. My car broke down. I was wondering if I could use your phone to call a tow truck. I forgot my phone this morning. I won't stay long as I need to be down there when my car is towed," Mike replied.

"Sure, come in Mike. You can use my phone. I have a phone directory as well, if you need it," I spoke.

"Thanks," Mike commented as he looked up the number for a towing company.

I was sure once again that Mike was lying to me about forgetting his phone. The Mike that I had known for years NEVER forgot it. What was happening now was not like my first time here, and I stood there, wondering what the real story was for him to want to visit me and my apartment. Mike was rich now and this apartment was not in the richer part of Newark. He did call a tow truck, though.

"Thanks, Rob," Mike said as he hung up the phone.

"You're welcome. You caught me by surprise this morning as you were the last person I expected to see standing at my door," I said with a chuckle.

"Yes, I am surprised as well. I have known all along

where you live, but with work and all, I have been extra busy and had no time to come here to visit," he responded.

"It's okay, Mike. What brought you to this area? It isn't the rich part of Newark," I spoke.

"I was headed home. I went to a club last night to have some fun. I ended up spending the night with a very nice young lady. As you know, I opted out of going to that dinner party. When I left her apartment this morning, I forgot to grab my phone. Now I need to go back there, to see if she has it or I need to get another one," Mike replied.

"That makes sense. If you get a new phone, give me your number for future use," I said.

"I will. I need to go now as the tow truck should be arriving soon," he commented.

"Okay. Thanks for dropping by," I replied as I unlocked the door for him to leave.

This was one story that I chose to believe. I knew what a drinker Mike was, and sometimes he was forgetful. He had told me that he would be going clubbing last night, and for once I believed that Mike had told me the truth. Then I had to laugh as that was a first for him.

I arrived at Steve and Nikki's home at 5:00 pm and was ready for my date. When I rang the doorbell, once again Steve answered the door.

"Come in, Robert," Steve said.

"Thanks, Steve. I am looking forward to taking Taylor out on a date tonight to dinner," I replied.

"She will be down in a minute as she is still getting ready. Would you like a glass of iced tea?" he asked.

"Yes, and thank you. We have really been having some hot weather lately," I remarked.

"We have and summer has just begun. Where are you taking Taylor tonight?" Steve asked.

"I am not sure yet, Steve. I am going to name off some different places that I know about and let Taylor decide which one she would like to go to," I replied.

"Taylor is easy to please and I am sure she will have a

good time, no matter where you take her," Steve spoke.

Before we could continue with our conversation, Taylor and Nikki came into the room. Taylor was gorgeous in the same gown once again that she had worn years ago. My heart melted!

"Would you like to finish your tea before we leave, Robert? If you do, it is okay with me," Taylor said.

"I almost have it drank, and then I will be ready to leave. I was just telling Steve that I have picked out some nice restaurants in the city to take you to. When we get in the car, I will let you decide which one you would like to eat at," I spoke.

"That would be wonderful, Robert. Thank you again for thinking of me," Taylor replied.

I really wanted to show Taylor that I was respectful of her and her wishes, unlike her husband Albert was. I didn't want to scare Taylor off by being too eager to be alone with her, but there was a part of my mind that told me that I should drop the tea the minute that I saw her and run out the door with her as fast as we could to leave, but then again, I also wanted to be respectful of Steve. He was my best friend and I didn't want to hurt his feelings. The old Robert from years ago didn't care whom he hurt as long as he got his way, but the new and improved Robert did care and was nothing like him.

I finished my tea and told Steve and Nikki that I would bring her back home later, in good shape. Of course, Steve laughed and said he trusted me with his life and he felt the same way when it came to Taylor. We were out the door and set to jet for a night of dinner and alone time.

I had told Taylor the different places where I would like to take her. They were elegant, but not as expensive as the places that I had taken her to before. Taylor told me to be the one to surprise her as she knew that she would enjoy it, no matter where we went. Then she smiled at me.

When we arrived at the restaurant, I went around to her side of the car and opened the door for her as I had done many years ago. I was a gentleman back then, and that is one quality that I didn't lose with my having the gold coin in my pocket, directing my life to the way that it should have been all along.

After we were seated in the restaurant, the waiter showed up and we ordered what we wanted to eat. At that moment, I could see that Taylor was a down-to-earth woman. She wasn't with me for how much money I had on me. We talked about everything we could think of to talk about as we sat across from each other at the table. I loved her eyes and loved her smile. She was easy to talk to, and I knew that she would be ready to go out again tomorrow night to another place for fun.

It looked to me like we were starting to connect, and this time there would be no story about Jenny as Jenny was married to Allen. I had no baggage that had followed me to Newark and no one that I was running from. I felt relaxed in our conversations, and this time I could be *me* and not the replica of Mike, the con artist, like I was years ago when it was Robert, the con artist.

We continued to talk and eat. After a few hours, it was time to take Taylor back to the house. I was certain that Steve would want me to come in and stay for a while to talk and drink more tea, and I was ready for this.

After we arrived at the house, before we went inside, I asked Taylor if she would like to go out again tomorrow night to dinner, and her answer was yes. At that moment we both smiled! I told her that I had to work and would be here to pick her up around 7:00 pm. She said that was fine and she would be ready to go when I arrived.

When we entered the house, Steve and Nikki were expecting us. Once again, all four of us sat on the couch with my drinking once again iced tea, and all of us talking. This night was a million times more special to me than years ago, when I felt the need to lie to Steve and not be a part of Taylor's family. I had been a selfish, self-centered, arrogant man at times, and I was very grateful that the old Robert was gone forever.

The next day I was patiently awaiting my time with Taylor that night. We had talked about many things the night before, and I was still waiting for her to tell me her story about her life with Albert. Until this happened, it would be a while before she felt comfortable enough around me to do this. As for me, I felt comfortable right from the start of seeing her again. She was my life, and as Kelly had told me many years ago when it came to Jenny, "Don't screw it up, Robert." I had no intentions of screwing this up!

That night, when I went to pick her up, Steve and Nikki were not there. They had gone to a competition to show my old truck, where it would be placed on display, front and center. I was proud of that truck and hoping that it took first place in the competition.

When I rang the doorbell, Taylor answered.

"Would you like to come in for some tea, Robert, before we leave?" she asked.

"No, thank you. I will pass this time. When we get to the restaurant, I will order some," I said.

"I'm ready to leave whenever you are," she commented.

"Let's go have some fun, Taylor. I know of a different nice restaurant to take you to. After we eat, if you would like to go see a movie, that is fine with me. If I'm not mistaken, there is a new movie out called *Chains*. I have heard good reviews about it. We can also share some popcorn," I responded with a smile.

"I would love to do this! Going to the movies has always been one of my favorite things to do," she spoke.

"There are also some clubs that have famous singers every night, if you would also like to do this sometime," I replied.

"That would be great, Robert. Thank you for thinking of me and trying so hard to make my time here in Newark enjoyable," Taylor spoke with a big smile.

"It is my pleasure to do this for you," I said.

We had arrived at the restaurant to eat, and from there

would go to the movies. I was hoping that she would lean her head against my shoulder, but I knew that it was too soon for this.

After the movie was over, she was so excited. She said that it had kept her on the edge of her seat from the start until the ending, and that she had the best time ever. That made me smile. I was doing everything right to make her life and her visit better, and this is what I wanted to do the rest of my life. Also, I wanted her to be able to see that I had a good heart, like she did years ago.

It was time to take her back home, and this night I didn't go into the house. I just walked her to the door and told her that I would pick her up the following night, and that I would be taking her to a club to see Celine Dion and Wayne Newton. Once again, she was very excited and told me that she had always wanted to see them, but couldn't get tickets as they were always sold out. I told her that she was about to get her opportunity and that I was excited as well. Then I told her good night and walked away. Things were going great once again between us.

That next night we went to the club, and when she saw Celine Dion sing, all she could do was sit there and smile. When Wayne Newton walked out on the stage and sang, I could see her smiling even bigger. Taylor was very happy, and this made me even happier. Like years ago, she was bubbling with excitement after we had left the club and she couldn't say enough about how much fun she had that night.

The following night when I picked her up after work, it was the same reaction when we went to see Mariah Carey perform. Taylor told me the same things that she had before. She was very grateful that she had finally, after many years of wanting to see not just Celine Dion and Wayne Newton, but also Mariah Carey in the same week. Her dreams were being fulfilled.

I had one more day of work until the weekend, and this time I would be taking her to see Cathedral Basilica of the Heart and the Yankee stadium. If we had enough time this weekend, we would also visit Princeton University as we had before. This would maybe happen on Saturday and Sunday. I knew that she had no memory of years ago because I had been taken back in time. All of what I was going through was a new beginning. With the help of the gold coin, it was as if many years ago when Robert, the con artist, that came here didn't exist with everything that I had done at that time.

All I knew was that I wanted to spend as much time with Taylor before her scheduled trip back to Chicago. With my not knowing for sure if she would have the same feelings again as she once had, all I could do was take her to the same places we visited before and show her love and respect like she deserved before we had even met. I wasn't sure what the coin had in store for me. I could even wake up tomorrow and be back in Apple Grove, or Kingston. Meanwhile, I was going to take it day by day and wait.

At last it was Saturday, and I was going to be able to spend two whole days with Taylor. I had told her that I would be over to get her at 9:00 a.m., and that we were going to tour the city to see the sights like she hadn't seen before. She was excited and so was I.

When she saw the Cathedral Basilica of the Heart, the only thing that she could say to me was "WOW!!!" This was an indication to me that she loved it. When we were finished seeing this, I took her to see the Yankee Stadium. Once again, she was amazed and told me that it was huge just like the Chicago Bears' stadium was. She said that if I ever went to Chicago, I should look her up. She would be the tour guide while I was there as she was having a wonderful time with me.

After she had seen Princeton University, Taylor told me that one of her uncles had gone to school there and that she had dreamed of seeing how big of a campus they had, and also the university itself. We had a wonderful day. I knew in my heart that this was just the beginning for us.

After we had eaten at a nice place again and talked as

we had done all day, it was time to take Taylor back to Steve and Nikki's home. It was late and Taylor and I were tired. I asked her to tell Steve that I would come in the house another time to talk. I walked Taylor to the front door and when I looked into her eyes and saw her smile, I could see that maybe she might be starting to have some feelings for me, but it was still too soon to really tell. This was the first long date that we had, and Taylor was a sensible woman. I knew that she wasn't going to act out her feelings before actually knowing whether they were real.

I told her good night as she opened the door and also said that I would be there at 9:00 a.m. the next morning, to get her again for another fun-filled day. Taylor thanked me for thinking of her and said that she would be ready when I arrived.

When I drove away, all I wanted to do was smile. I couldn't wait until I got to hold her in my arms once again.

The next day was Sunday, and if time repeated itself, Taylor would be waiting for me to drive up so that she could walk out the front door of the mansion. Her explanation for doing this would be the same one as she had given before.

When I arrived there and had parked, I was correct as Taylor was dressed casually, and after hearing my car she walked over to meet me. I got out and opened the passenger door for her. When she got in, she told me the same thing she did years ago, and history had repeated itself as it was the same answer. She didn't want to wake anyone up.

After eating breakfast, we were on our way to see the Newark Museum. With my knowing that she worked for a museum in Chicago, I was sure that she would enjoy seeing the art work that was displayed at this one. The first time that we had gone there, Taylor was very impressed. She loved everything that she had seen.

Our day went fast and I had two more weeks before Taylor would fly back home. I had to show her just how much she meant to me, with little time left to do it in. I could see that we were getting closer when I looked into her eyes.

When I took Taylor back to the house, I once again went inside to talk with Steve and Nikki. It was good to be able to spend time with them as well. As I looked at Nikki, she had a smile on her face. I could see that she knew in her heart that Taylor was falling for me and that she was okay with that.

Steve and I talked about a fishing trip that he was planning next year. He wanted to include me in it. I told him that I would love to go with him. After a while, it was time for me to leave, to once again go back to an empty apartment. Maybe someday Taylor would be staying there with me, or in a house of our own. I had no way of knowing where our life would take us after she left to go back home. If things did work out for us, I would be the one flying back from Chicago the night of Taylor's death. This time there would be no meeting for me to want to attend out of being greedy. If the plane crashed, it would have me on board and not Taylor. I would save her life and give up my own.

—12—

NEW BEGINNING OR SAD ENDING?

Every night for the next five days was filled with more fun after I was done with work for the day. Taylor and I had gone to just about every fancy restaurant in Newark. Once again, like years ago, she said that she wanted to see the movie, *Bear Country*. After we had walked out of the theater, she told me again the story of how she always wanted to visit Colorado.

I knew that this coming weekend would be the time that she would share with me the story of the life she had with Albert. I would have no story to share with her about Jenny, and me. If this did happen, I would be sympathetic like I was years ago, and show her that I did care about her and the way that she had been mistreated by him.

Because I wasn't working for Heatherton Incorporated this time around, with me working construction instead, I had shorter working hours and was able to take her more places than the last time. So far, she didn't put her head on my shoulder like before or hold my hand. This would come tomorrow, when I picked her up at the house again for a day of fun. It was the beginning of the second weekend. My time with her here was getting shorter.

Saturday morning, I was at Steve and Nikki's home early to get Taylor for another long day of fun. Today we would be going to see the Bronx Zoo and Six Flags. Taylor was dressed more casually and so was I. Of course, she loved all the animals at the zoo, and we yelled and screamed on the rides at Six Flags. Our day went by quickly with a lot of talking as I wanted her to get to know this Robert Stone, to see if she accepted me like she had the Robert Stone, con artist.

The next Saturday would be the day that Taylor would take her flight back to Chicago. I had tomorrow with her for a long day of fun and more talking. I was going to make the best of it. After that, the coin would decide if our story together turned out good, or if I would wake up in a different place and town, needing to repair more damage that I had done in my life. The gold coin was in charge!

Sunday, after I arrived at the house, Taylor was on her way out the door. I got out of the car and this time, instead of waiting for her to hold my hand first like she did the first time around, I grabbed her hand to walk her to the car. I wasn't sure if it was too soon to show her any kind of affection, but I was taking a chance, and one that I hoped I didn't regret later. Instead of her jerking her hand away from mine, she continued to hold onto it and smiled at me. I could see then that she had feelings for me, and that this day and the days to follow were going to allow me to hold Taylor in my arms again. I was so happy!

That day we went to Bushkill Falls after I took her out to eat. There we walked around talking, laughing and enjoying everything that we had seen. Then we went to the Branch Brook Park. This was where, years ago, Taylor had decided to tell me the story of herself and Albert. She had the cook prepare a cooler full of food once again for us. Not long after she laid the blanket down on the ground and we had eaten, we laid down to talk.

This day Taylor did tell me her story. After she had finished, I told her the same thing that I did years ago, minus the Jenny story, and Taylor could see my heart. I admitted to her that I was having feelings for her and that I felt like

I always would.

Instead of waiting like I did years ago, kissing her at Steve and Nikki's front door, I went ahead like I wanted to back then and kissed her there in the park. Taylor said that, like me, she too was having feelings for me and that she wasn't sure where we should go next with them. When I kissed her, I felt like I had died and gone to Heaven. My heart was full of so much love for this woman. I had waited a lifetime to be able to do this.

That day we talked more and laughed harder and longer than we had before. I held her in my arms and we held hands as we kissed. It was time for me to take her back to the house and I didn't want to let her go. I knew I had only four days left to spend with her, to convince her this time to stay with me and not to return to Chicago. If she did return, once again we would be flying back and forth to see each other until either the end or the beginning of a new life together. I didn't know if I could change the course that had happened before years ago, but I was going to give it everything I had inside me to undo what had happened. I didn't want this to be the end of the story of our life together.

The next day and every day after that for the rest of the week until Friday, Taylor and I went out to eat and went to my apartment to talk and hold each other. She had found my dirty sock, like she did years ago, and it was a repeat of the laughter that we had once had. As we held onto each other and kissed, neither one of us wanted to say goodbye. We had discussed her staying here, but because Taylor was a sensible woman, she wanted to go back to Chicago to work until we had the right amount of time to decide exactly where our feelings were for one another.

I agreed with her as I had before, knowing what the outcome could be for us if history repeated itself again. I just knew that our last visit years ago, when I asked her to fly here, and she was killed in a plane crash, wasn't going to happen this time. I was going to make sure of that. There would be no stopping me unless the coin had a different direction for me to go.

It had allowed me to go back in time to fix all the mistakes that I had made, with the exception of when I was a stock broker and took money from innocent people. I was sure that the millions of dollars that I had sitting in a bank account in Apple Grove was no longer there and had been returned to the rightful people that it should have gone to in the first place. This made me smile as most of it was stolen. I had worked hard for what I had here in Newark this time. I was very grateful to the coin for not giving up on me, and continually wanting to stay with me until the end.

When Thursday night came and Taylor announced that she was going to spend the next day with Steve and Nikki, my heart sunk. I felt sadder than I had felt in many years. Our last kiss and hug continued at the front door of the house, and like many years ago, we didn't want to let go of each other. Our love for one another wasn't lust and we were sure that it was love. There had been no sexual interaction between us. Taylor and I just needed love from the heart, and this is what we had together, hopefully for the rest of our lives.

I drove away that night, wondering what our future would bring for us. I knew that when Taylor went into the house, she was wondering the same thing. The next day, she did spend her time with her aunt and uncle. On Saturday morning, I did try calling her, and like before she had already gotten on the plane and left.

For the next six months, we continued to fly back and forth to see each other. She had fallen deeply in love with me as I already did with her years ago. The day that I had asked her to fly here to see me before was going to be different. I would be the one on the plane going there to see her, not knowing if I was going to be the one to die in that crash.

With Steve telling me years ago that I should have been the one that did die, I didn't know if I would ever see Taylor again once I got on that plane to return to Newark. I took the engagement ring, and she had agreed to marry me, stating that she would be very happy to be my wife. She said that she knew that her uncle and aunt would be very happy for both of us. Taylor also stated that she knew that we were going to have a long beautiful future together in Newark.

Even though I didn't know my outcome that night, I stood there and smiled at her. We held each other for a long time before I had to board the plane. When we had our last kiss, I wasn't sure if it would be the last time that my lips touched hers. When I looked into her beautiful eyes, I saw happiness. When I walked away from her for maybe the last time, I turned around to look at her. I threw her a kiss. She caught it and put her hand next to her heart. She did the same thing to me. I also caught it, closed my hand, and put it next to my heart.

We were connected, whether it be for the rest of our lives or just for the short time that we had together. I knew that it wasn't up to the gold coin to decide my fate. It was up to God. All I could do when I got on the plane was pray that this wouldn't be the end of me and the end of a beautiful lifetime with Taylor.

As I was sitting on the plane, praying, the pilot announced that we would be landing at the Newark airport shortly and to fasten our seat belts as we were in for a bumpy ride. I was not only thinking about Taylor, but also thinking about Mother, Father, Pam and Carl. I knew that all of them would be fine if I did die that night. I sat there with my eyes closed, waiting to see when the plane touched down, if it skidded off the runway as it had done many years ago with Taylor and the other passengers on board.

The pilot was right as the weather was bad and there was no turning back as it would be a matter of seconds, and I would then know my fate. I felt the wheels touch down as I continued to keep my eyes closed. Whatever my outcome was, I had made it right with Taylor, Steve, Nikki and myself. I had no guilt. Also, I had made good choices this time around and had no regrets with the changes that I had made.

My life was good, and I was very thankful for the opportunity that I had to go back in time to redo what I had messed up the first time.

I knew that the man sitting next to me was wondering why I continued to pray while I was on the plane, and why I had my eyes shut when we were getting ready to land. He had no idea what his fate might be as well.

When the plane came to a complete stop, I opened my eyes and we were sitting at the gate where we were supposed to be. All of us were still alive and I sat in my seat and took a deep breath. It wasn't my time to die. All I wanted to do was smile. I gave the man next to me a big hug. He hugged me back, but gave me a funny look. I am sure that his thoughts were that this was the first time that I had flown and that I was terrified of the plane ride. The truth being known, I was very grateful that every one of us on that plane was alive!

After I entered the airport, the first thing I did was call Taylor, Nikki and Steve. I told them that I was alive and couldn't wait until the wedding. All of them laughed at me, not knowing what I knew had happened years ago, and said, "Of course you are alive, Robert!"

Taylor decided to move to Newark. She had quit her job and moved in with me. It wasn't long after that when we had the wedding of our dreams. There were hundreds of people who were there to share the big day with us. I finally got to meet Taylor's father and mother. Her father was the one who gave her away as her mother sat there, crying. I wasn't sure at the time if her mother was crying because of Taylor getting married or the fact that she was marrying a poor man, like her sister Nikki had when she married Steve.

Steve, and Nikki sat in their seat and cheered when Taylor and I were pronounced husband and wife. They had and always would be a big part of Taylor's and my life together. My mother, father, Pam and Carl had also come to Newark to be a part in our joyous union in marriage for the rest of our lives. Mother and Father continued to visit us as we did them, until they both had passed away.

Steve and Nikki lived a long life as well. They had moved from Newark to Colorado when they retired, so that they could live close to Taylor, Kilo, Kara and I. Steve loved to fish and we had some great fishing trips. Steve was my best friend and continued to be until he took his last breath.

Nikki and Taylor were like mother and daughter, and also continued to be very close. Carl had finally grown up after many years of being the odd man out. Pam and her husband had started a family, like Taylor and I did, and continued to live in Florida. When Taylor changed her mind about having children, she told me that she felt as if the reason why she didn't want children before was because of everything that had happened to her when she was married to Albert. I told her that my thoughts had changed as well, and that I couldn't wait to be a father

The day in the delivery room was a moment in time when we both held onto one another again. When our son Kilo was born and we heard him cry for the first time, we both had tears of joy running down our faces. When Kara was born, it was the same feeling.

As for Mike, it wasn't long after I had landed that last time in Newark when he had decided to go back to Kingston. I knew that he loved the money that he had made, but like me, he was getting older and wanted to move west again to live out the rest of his life, or maybe instead he felt like there could be some heat coming down on him soon and he needed to get out of the city of Newark. At that time, only Mike knew what really was going on with him.

After Taylor and I moved to Colorado, Mike and I weren't living in the same town or city again, but once in a while he would still call me, or I would call him. Even as we continued to age, Mike didn't change. He was still the con artist/player that he had been his whole life.

Taylor and I had been given a complete life together as we had dreamed about. The gold coin continued to stay with me. I kept wondering if it was because both of us had shared so much together, or maybe because it wanted to make sure that I stayed on the straight and narrow. Whatever the reason behind it was, I was still forever grateful that the coin decided to give me a second chance.

Time passed by too quickly and Taylor and I were in our 80s. We had a good life together and didn't regret one day of all the years that we had spent with each other.

Today I am lying in a hospital bed as Taylor is talking to our doctor. She had told him the story of my life and hers during the time that Robert, the con artist, first met her, and the time I had with Jenny before David was born, and the second life that I had been allowed to have to undo bad choices that I had made when the gold coin took me back in time. The look on the doctor's face is either out of disbelief or denial.

"Taylor, this story that you just told me sounds unbelievable! Are you sure that Robert just didn't make this story up?" the doctor asked.

"I choose to believe him. I know that this story sounds like something that only a person with a big imagination would make up, but in all the years that I have known Robert, he has been truthful with me. He wanted his story to be known to me and how my life and his had been spared the second time. I know that we are just two old people now, Doctor, that might be forgetful, or get confused, but in this case, everything that I told you is true. Robert and I both know that there is a good chance that he might not be going home today. Doctor, we have had a wonderful life together and what happens now we both accept." Taylor spoke.

"Okay, Taylor. I am still questioning the story, but I am confused why you chose to tell it to me today of all days," the doctor replied.

"Because, Doctor, Robert wanted you to know about this because he can't tell you this story himself. He also wanted me to tell you that even though you have a different way of thinking than we do about how we got here on this planet, and what happens next, that there is always a chance of being able to go back in time to fix what anyone messes up the first time in their lives. Our choices in our lives are our own, as everyone knows this, but sometimes like the gold coin coming into Robert's life, proves that there is always a way to undo a mistake that a person makes, with or without a gold coin.

"I know that all of this that I told you is overwhelming, and with you being a doctor, you find it hard to believe as you have been taught things that you believe to be real. We are not sure what tomorrow will bring for us. We also know that for every action that we have made throughout our life, here has been a reaction because of our choices. If we both walk out of here to return to our home, it will be because we are supposed to as the gold coin can't change our destiny any longer. Think about what I said, Doctor, and always make good choices as you might not find a gold coin someday. It might be all up to you," Taylor responded.

"*Wow!* You have given me something to think about! This is one conversation that I will NEVER forget!" the doctor spoke.

At that time the nurse came into the room where Taylor, the doctor and I were, to see if I could have a visitor. The doctor said that I could and, for the first time in years, Mike entered the room. Taylor had called Mike to tell him to come to the hospital. Mike still had a cocky smile and attitude. He spoke to Taylor and also me. When Taylor opened her hand, the gold coin had disappeared. She then asked Mike what time it was and he reached into his pocket to pull out his watch to see.

With his watch, he also pulled out the gold coin. Mike looked at it as the doctor, Taylor and I did. Mike said, "What is this doing in my pocket?"

At that moment it was flashing again, and brighter than it had been for many years. Taylor and the doctor looked at me and smiled. At that time, the doctor did believe my story and he was smiling to let me know that he did.

None of us told Mike about the coin and what he was about to experience himself. He would know in time, with the help of the flashing gold coin that would NEVER leave him until its job was done.

THE END

Other Books by Jana Nolan

THE OLD HENDERSON MINE

MIND POWER

SOUNDS OF FEAR

SECRETS OF SLEEPING INDIAN MOUNTAIN

PURE VENGEANCE

THE UNEXPLAINABLE

DEPRIVATION

Visit her Author Web site at
JanaNolan.com